OUTNUMBERED

HER ROYAL HAREM: EMBER
BOOK TWO

CATHERINE BANKS

TURBO KITTEN INDUSTRIES

HER ROYAL HAREM

EMBER

2

OUTNUMBERED

USA TODAY BESTSELLING AUTHOR
CATHERINE BANKS

CHAPTER
ONE

"Why does it hurt so much?" I gasped as I lay on my back on the ground and tried to catch my breath. Each time I inhaled, I winced in pain and felt like my ribs were on fire.

"Because you're fighting the magic instead of working with it," Nico, King of the Mages explained, gripped my hand, and pulled me up to my feet.

"It's not going where I want it to," I grumbled and dusted myself off. I was trying really hard to learn to create a shield, a magical dome-shaped barrier that would protect me and whoever was inside of it from attack.

"You're getting better each session, Ember. Don't get too upset." He patted my shoulder and we turned, heading towards the house.

Outside the front door stood Caleb, King of Hybrids, Prince of the Mages, Dragons, Elves, Sirens, and Wolves, and one of my boyfriends and pack members. He had his hands in his pockets, one leg bent with the foot resting on the doorframe behind him, and a soft smile on his face as he watched me. Tall, muscular, handsome, and more powerful than I think any of us wanted to accept, he was everything you'd expect a royal to be. The late twenty-year-old male was a specimen of masculine perfection.

My breath caught every time I saw him and my wrist tingled where his mark was. A sign that I was his and that also kept unwanted males from bothering me.

"Breakfast is ready," he announced as we approached, kissed my cheek as I walked by, and followed us into the house.

The giant cottage mansion was owned by his parents, Princess Jolie of the Sirens, King Nico of the Mages, Prince Rhys of the Dragons, Prince Foxfire of the Elves, and Prince Deryn of the Werewolves. It was a place we frequented, especially for training sessions like today.

"Great, I am starving," I said, hurried into the dining room, and sat beside Triston, a hybrid mage-shifter who took the form of a tiger, and another one of my boyfriends and packmates.

He kissed my cheek and put food on my plate. "Did you have a good training session?"

"I don't feel like I learned more, but Nico said I'm doing better."

"Practice is key," Triston reminded me. "I've been doing more mage training as well and it's not nearly as easy as shifting."

"Speaking of shifting," Deryn said as he walked into the dining room, a piece of paper in his hand. He shook it over his head, smiling. "I finally found your birth certificate."

My fork clanked against my plate loudly as I dropped it and rushed over to try to get the paper from him.

Caleb was faster and snatched it out of his father's hand.

Deryn growled.

Caleb's eyes widened and then he started laughing so hard, he bent over and clutched his stomach, the paper sticking out.

I took the paper from him, nearly ripping it in my haste, and read my birth name: EmberRew Rockwood.

"Rew? Like ... a red eyed white rabbit?" I squeaked.

Caleb slapped the dining table as he continued to laugh and nodded with tears flowing down his face.

My elven animal form was supposed to be ... a rabbit.

"What's wrong with a rabbit?" Nico asked as he took a seat at the table.

Jolie, Caleb's mother, walked in. "Rabbit? What? What did I miss?"

I handed her the birth certificate and walked to my seat, shoving a big bite of food in my mouth with a frown. Really? A rabbit?

"Your name is cute," Jolie said. "And how interesting that your debut into royal society was with a red dress." She winked, trying to lighten my mood.

"Jolie, I'm a prey animal dating predators. What is that supposed to mean? Is it an omen? Is it a sign that this connection isn't what we think it is?"

She pursed her lips. "No, Ember. It doesn't mean anything like that. It's just who you are. Does this change how you feel about her?" Her question was aimed at Caleb and Triston.

"Of course not," Triston said and put more fruit on my plate. "Just means we know her animal form now."

"No," Caleb said and sat on my other side, kissing my cheek. "It just makes her even more adorable. I can't wait for you to shift so I can tweak that adorable bunny nose." He pinched the tip of my nose and I smacked his hand away, giving him a stern glare that only made him smile wider. His bright blue eyes full of mirth.

This was unfair. A bunny? Why? Why did my parents name me after a bunny? Why couldn't they have named me after a puma or something? Something predatory!

"Maybe I don't have that form anyway," I countered. "Maybe I'm not a shifter. Not all elves are shifters."

"That is true," Fox said as he walked in. "Not all of us shift, but I can tell you with certainty that you have a second form."

"How?" I asked, genuinely curious.

"Caleb told me," he said.

I turned to look at Caleb. "How do you know?"

He shoved a huge piece of food into his mouth and shrugged.

"Caleb," I growled, the sound so deep that I gasped immediately and put a hand to my mouth.

"Oh, that was *hot*," Caleb praised. "When did you learn that? Who are you channeling? Was it Branson?"

Speaking of Branson. "Where is he?" I asked, looking around.

"Dad recruited him for a job," Deryn answered. Deryn's father was King Daniel of the Werewolves. He'd taken a liking to Branson and even though Branson turned into a bear, he found Branson had werewolf blood and pulled him into the werewolf clan.

"Oh," I said and frowned, "maybe I am channeling him. I was irritated, but haven't been able to growl like that before." When I'd met Caleb, we had discovered that we had a connection, one unlike anything they'd heard of before. And not just him, but I had a connection with Triston, Branson, and Riddick. Branson and Caleb had marked me, which had strengthened the connection even more and now I randomly channeled aspects of them. My siren blood also meant our emotions got entangled as well.

I didn't like it, but it amused Caleb immensely.

"Caleb, how do you know I can shift?" I asked again, bringing us back to the topic at hand.

"Your eyes have shifted before," he answered after drinking some milk.

"What?" I breathed. When had that happened? Why? How? Had that ever happened before, or was it just part of the marking and connection?

He nodded. "A few times, but the first time was when you cured all the cursed beings in the park."

That was before the marking, so that ruled that part out and the connection had been weak and new then as well.

"Oh," I whispered and poked at the food on my plate.

"Do you want me to work with you on shifting?" Caleb asked.

My eyes narrowed. "No."

"I'll teach her," Fox said. "You're going to tease her too much."

Caleb frowned. "I know when to be serious."

Everyone at the table laughed or scoffed.

His eyes narrowed and I could feel his anger.

"Son, you handle a lot of things very well, but when it comes to Ember, you tease her quite often," Jolie said, trying to soften the tension in the room.

"How many bunny jokes would you make during training?" I asked him.

His lip twitched and he sighed. "Fine, you're right."

"Now that training is over, why don't we head to the apartments and play some games," Triston suggested.

"Wait!" Jolie shouted. "I have important news."

Caleb and I both frowned, knowing her news was likely something we wouldn't like.

She stood and said, "We've decided to take a vacation."

Caleb blinked. "What? You don't take vacations."

She scoffed. "Don't I know it, but now that you're grown and have your own pack, we've decided to take a week to enjoy ourselves. We're going to leave next Monday and will be gone for seven full days."

"So, no training for seven days?" I asked, excitement making my mouth drop and eyes widen.

"That hurts, Ember. Straight to the heart," Nico said and pressed a hand to his heart.

"Seven days of freedom!" Caleb shouted and raised his hands over his head, pumping his fists in the air.

"Yeah!" Triston shouted and slapped his palms against Caleb's.

"If you were living at home, I would ground you right now for being disrespectful," Fox said.

"We love you all, but it's been a very stressful month,"

Caleb explained. "We've been training like the apocalypse is upon us. We need a break."

"You get a break when we dismantle the H.E.," Nico said sternly.

I flinched, feeling like I was somehow responsible for my adoptive parents' and their creation of a terrible organization bent on destroying my kind.

Caleb reached over and intertwined our fingers. "We know how important it is, Dad. You don't have to remind us."

Nico sighed and ran a hand down his face. "Sorry, it's been a bad morning already. Caleb, come talk with me in the study." He stood, kissed Jolie on the cheek, and headed out of the dining room.

Caleb snagged a piece of fruit off my plate and winked. "Duty calls, bunny girl. I'll be back soon."

Snarling, I flung a piece of cantaloupe towards him, but the quick bastard just caught it and stuffed it into his mouth.

"Eat more," Triston ordered and put another spoonful of scrambled eggs on my plate. "You've not been eating enough."

"My ribs hurt," I complained.

"Eat the eggs and then when we get home I'll make you a smoothie," he said, trying to offer me something I would enjoy as a treat.

"Strawberry?" I asked.

He winked. "Of course."

Within seconds I'd shoveled the eggs into my mouth and swallowed them down. "Okay."

Jolie shook her head. "The more time I spend with you, the more you remind me of me."

"Which only worries us," Fox said. "We know how much trouble you were, how often danger was attracted to you, and if that amount follows Ember, our poor son is going to be wrought with attacks and angst."

"Wow," she said, drawing the word out. "Is this attack Jolie and Ember day? Did I miss the memo?"

"Right!" I shouted. "I came here to train and now I'm getting teased and attacked."

"You know what! No. Come on, Ember." She set her fork down, walked to me, pulled me from my seat, and tugged me towards the door. "We're having a girls' day. You lot can fend for yourselves, or I guess have a relaxing day without harbingers of destruction around you."

"Jolie," Fox crooned, "that's not what we meant."

She bared her teeth. "No. You. Are. Burnt."

With a snap of her fingers, she and I teleported out of the house and into the middle of Leona's house.

Leona sat up with a start from the couch where she'd been reading a magazine on her couch. "Uh, hi."

"Girls' day," Jolie growled.

Jolie's eyes brightened. She leapt to her feet, grabbed her purse, and rushed over to grab Jolie's hand. "Yes!"

CHAPTER
TWO

Girls' day apparently meant mani-pedis, tea with small sandwiches and scones, a shopping trip at a dress boutique, and lunch at a high-scale restaurant where we didn't even have to wait to be seated. Talk about epic!

"This has been the best day ever," I told them as I sipped on my mimosa and stroked a hand down my new dress. It was a sunny yellow maxi dress with thin shoulder straps that tied into a bow and had a slit up both sides of my legs up to my thighs.

Jolie and Leona nodded their agreement as they drank their mimosas. They also wore new dresses, and all of us had matching pink flip flops with rhinestones along the straps. Leona had also purchased us all matching silver heart necklaces.

"There are times it's essential to get away," Jolie said.

"You never did tell me what happened," Leona said.

"They were picking on us," I answered.

"I *may* have overreacted a little, but I'm pretty sure that was Rhys's fault since he was at his parents' at that time and was likely irritated with one of his family members." Jolie shrugged. "It worked out in the end."

"Why were they picking on you?" Leona asked me.

"We found out my birth name."

Her eyes widened and she gasped. "What's your name? What's your animal?"

I groaned and dropped my head to the table. "Bunny."

"What?" she asked.

"EmberRew is her birthname," Jolie said.

"That is *adorable!* Why are you acting like it's awful?"

Lifting my head I said, "Leona, I'm a bunny dating carnivores." I took a drink of my mimosa to soothe myself.

She smirked. "Those men already eat you. What are you worried about?"

I nearly spit out my drink and started coughing.

"Don't kill my future daughter-in-law, Leona," Jolie said and patted my back.

Grabbing my napkin, I wiped my mouth and shook my head. "You two always catch me off guard with your comments."

"You'll get used to it," Leona said with a single shrug of her shoulder.

I was completely ignoring Jolie's comment, not even wanting to acknowledge it.

"So, EmberRew, have you tried shifting yet?" Leona asked.

"No."

"Fox offered to teach her," Jolie added.

"What about me?" a smooth male voice asked beside us.

Leona looked over her shoulder as I turned to see who it was.

Silverowl, one of Leona's mates, Prince of the Elves, and Fox's brother, smiled at us. "I apologize for interrupting your day, but my lovely mate mysteriously vanished from our house and I was worried she might have been dragged into mischief by a certain princess." His eyes darted to Jolie and his smile widened.

"I think today really is pick on Jolie day," she muttered.

"What about you?" Leona asked Silverowl.

He walked around to her right side, kissed her cheek, and said, "I can teach Ember to shift."

"You want to teach her?" Leona asked, blinking rapidly.

"I feel like I haven't been holding up my end of this relationship. I am Caleb's uncle and I should assist with training his pack just like the others have been."

All of Leona's other mates had been helping train us in some aspect, so his statement did make sense, but we all knew he was the busiest of them.

Setting my drink down, I smiled at him. "I appreciate your offer, but I wouldn't want to take up a lot of your time. You are running like four businesses and have duties as prince, too."

"I think it's a great idea," Leona said. "He needs a break from some of the businesses and he's better at teaching than Fox."

"That settles it then. I'll meet you tomorrow morning after your fighting training is completed," he said with a nod.

"Okay." Now that we were doing it, I felt nervous. What if I couldn't shift?

"What's your name?" he asked.

"EmberRew," Leona answered for me. "Isn't it adorable?"

"EmberRew, how interesting," he said and tapped his chin in thought. "Most times we don't pick a name so specific as to the color of the animal."

Picking my mimosa back up, I let my mind wander to thoughts of next week, when we'd not be training. Would we just hang out? Go somewhere ourselves? I really wanted to travel. To see more of the world.

"Ember," Silverowl said, drawing my attention back to him. "I have homework for you."

I blinked. "Silverowl, I'm twenty-eight. What do you mean homework?"

He smiled. "It's simple, promise. Before tomorrow, I want you to make a list of ten reasons why being a rabbit shifter is actually an advantage."

"Really?" I asked. "How is that going to help?"

"Just trust me, please," he said.

"Fine," I exhaled.

"Alright, I'll leave you three to your day." He set Leona's phone on the table beside her, kissed her cheek, and left.

"Now that he's gone, let's talk about next week," Leona said.

"Next week?" I asked.

"While Jolie and her men are gone, how would you feel about coming to my house for a sleepover? You and your entire pack."

My mouth dropped and I gasped. "Really?"

She nodded. "I think it'll be good for you to see how a group

like mine interacts, plus it'll give me more time to truly assess
your siren abilities and see if you need training in other areas I
don't notice when we only have a few hours a day together."

"Sounds great," I said with a smile.

"Plus, you're going to be bored without me around and
need someone to entertain you, right?" Jolie asked with a
smirk.

"Shut up," Leona grumbled.

Jolie and I laughed, knowing she was right.

"So, do you guys want to help me with my homework?" I
asked with a smile and put my hands together as I begged.
"Please."

"Nope," Jolie and Leona replied immediately, both
making the p sound pop.

I groaned and went to take a drink only to realize it was
empty. Glaring at the empty glass, like it was the glass's
fault.

"Would you like a refill, ma'am?" a waiter asked.

I looked up and my eyes nearly bulged out of my head.
The guy was quite possibly the most attractive man I had
ever seen. Surpassing Caleb, Riddick, and Caleb's fathers.

Jolie and Leona smirked, which made me blush.

"Yes, please," I requested and held out my glass.

His finger brushed mine and a shock went through me,
making me hiss and drop the glass, but he caught it before it
hit the ground with preternatural speed. "My apologies," he
whispered and bowed his head before raising his eyes to
meet mine, a frown crossing his gorgeous features before he
spun around and hurried away.

"Oh, you are lucky my boy wasn't here just now," Jolie teased me.

"Shut up," I snapped. "You can't tell me he isn't gorgeous."

"Oh, he was gorgeous, but far too young for us," Jolie said.

Leona scoffed. "Speak for yourself, old lady."

"Can I be honest with you two and not have you rat me out to my pack?" I asked softly, clenching my hands in my lap.

"Always," Jolie said with a nod.

"What if I have some connection with other hybrids? What if it's not just my current pack?" My heart started fluttering as soon as I asked.

"Are you worried there will be more males you're connected to?" Leona asked.

I nodded.

"Because you think it will upset your current males?" Jolie asked.

"Because it's already insane that there are four men wanting a joint relationship with me," I admitted.

Both smiled softly and reached across the table to set their hand on mine.

"Sweetheart, it's going to be okay," Jolie whispered.

"Would it be so bad if one or two more came into your life?" Leona asked. "Especially gorgeous ones?"

"Did you forget that I've been a hermit in the woods?" I asked.

"You're far too social to have continued that life. I don't even know how you did it for so long as it was. Perhaps because you had the patients to treat and you could talk to animals?" Jolie tapped her lips. "Is that an elf or a siren ability?" She looked at Leona.

"I don't know of any sirens who can talk to animals and make them smarter," she said. "But we also know that a lot of our history and knowledge is missing." She shrugged. "Who knows? Perhaps Ember is the next level siren!"

"Okay, back to reality," I said and laughed. "I don't want to mess things up with my pack, they're great and we're still learning about each other. Adding more people, even one, would be ... hectic."

"Darlin', your life has been nothing *but* hectic since you uncovered your connection with Caleb and Riddick. I don't see that slowing down anytime soon." Jolie patted my hand and both leaned back.

"Your mimosa," the hot waiter said, bowing as he set it in front of me. "I'll go get your meals now as well, but is there anything else I can grab on the way?"

With him so close, I realized I could sense him, similar to Riddick. I chugged half of my mimosa and looked away from him to try to distract myself.

"Another round for all three of us," Jolie said, trying and failing to hide her smile.

Glancing out of the corner of the eye, I saw him swallow hard, nod, smile, and say, "Of course, Princess. I'll be back quickly."

Hanging my head in shame, I walked behind Jolie into the house, the hot waiter's phone number saved in my cell. I still wasn't quite sure how it had happened, but it had.

"That is a lovely dress," Triston said and stood from the couch where he and Riddick were watching Caleb and Fox play a videogame.

"Thanks," I said, eyes down and nerves making my heart race.

"What's wrong?" he asked as he approached me, set his hands on my arms, and rubbed up and down.

"Um, I—"

"Caleb, come talk to me," Jolie ordered him and walked out of the room.

He set his controller down, looked at me with an arched brow, and followed after his mother.

"Want to try to shift?" Fox asked.

"About that ..." How did I tell him? Screw it, I'd just come right out and tell him. We were all adults and I didn't need to sugarcoat things. "Uh, Silverowl found us at the restaurant and he offered to teach me to shift."

Fox gasped and smiled wide. "He's finally taking an interest, huh? Good for him."

"So, you're not upset?" I asked.

He shook his head. "As long as you have a good instructor, I don't care if it's me or someone else."

"Thanks," I said and breathed in relief.

"Ready go home after Caleb is done talking to Jolie?" Riddick asked.

I nodded. "I need a nap."

"Eventful morning?" Caleb asked, a neutral expression on his face that worried me as he returned from talking to Jolie and joined us in the foyer.

"Yes."

The expression shifted and he smiled and draped an arm across my shoulders. "Then let's get you home."

The drive to the apartments was tense and Caleb stared out the passenger window without talking the entire way. Completely unlike him. I wanted to ask what Jolie had told him, but wanted to wait until we were at the apartments first. Not that I didn't trust Ezio, but me telling them about the waiter was our pack's matter and I didn't want to bring that up without being alone.

"Thanks for driving us," I said and waved to Ezio as I climbed out.

"Call if you want to go anywhere," he said and returned my wave.

Once inside the foyer, I turned to Caleb and asked, "Did she tell you?"

He returned to the neutral expression. "Tell me what?"

Sighing, I said, "When we were at lunch, the waiter touched my hand and there was a spark. He gave me his phone number."

Triston asked, "Another hybrid?"

I nodded.

"You think it's a connection like we have?" Caleb asked. His neutral expression had me wondering what he was actually feeling, what emotions were going through him? His hands were in his pants pockets and he looked relaxed, but that didn't mean he wasn't upset.

I didn't think anything was quite like the connection I had with the four of them. "It was a similar type pull," I said and looked down at my feet.

"Is he attractive?"

Flinching, I asked, "Why does that matter?"

"That's a yes," Triston said and chuckled.

"Are you going to call him?" Caleb asked.

Sliding my hands into my hair, I gripped it at the scalp and groaned. "I don't know! I don't know how to handle any of this! I don't want you mad at me. I don't want to have so many connections. Life was so much simpler when I was a hermit!"

Turning, I ran up the stairs, ignoring their calls. I opened my apartment door, but two hands slammed against it on either side of my head, keeping it closed and caging me in.

"Take a breath, sweetheart," Caleb ordered, his mouth

beside my ear, making the hair move with his breath and sending a shiver down my spine.

Obeying, I took a shuddering breath, hand still grasping the door handle.

"Why are you so upset?" he asked.

"Because you're angry," I whispered.

"No."

"No?" Spinning around, I came face to face with him.

His eyes dropped to my mouth before going back to my eyes. "I'm not angry."

"Liar," I accused.

His lips twitched, but didn't go into a full smile. "I'm irritated, yes, about the situation, but I am not angry at you or with you."

"Huh?" He wasn't making sense.

Dropping his head, he rested his forehead against mine and our connection tingled at the contact and my heart slowed as I relaxed a bit. "I'm sorry I made you think I was mad at you. I'm irritated that there might be more hybrids you have a connection to because it means sharing you with even more people, and I feel like I barely get time with you as it is. Plus, it means I need to find this hybrid and see if he is supposed to be part of my pack. The fact that there are hybrids who I should have recognized or found and brought into my pack, but you're the one finding them bothers me. What kind of king am I to not notice my own people?"

So it wasn't just about me, it was his worry about being a good leader.

Wrapping my arms around his waist, I hugged him tight and said, "You're doing the best you can and we all know part of the issue is your need to stay in this city while training me to ensure I am ready to travel. If I weren't a hindrance, you would be out there finding the hybrids and doing what you were before you met me."

"You aren't a hindrance," he said and shook his head.

"Come inside, please," I begged. "Stay with me for a bit."

He scooped me up into his arms and buried his nose against my neck. "Yes, my queen."

"I'm not a queen." I giggled, liking the way it sounded coming from his lips, though.

He didn't respond, just carried me inside, locked my door behind us, and lay on the couch with me, letting me lay my head on his chest.

"Too many clothes," I hissed and stood.

Instead of teasing me, he sat up and removed his shit, then held his arms open again for me.

Laying back down, I rubbed my face against his bare chest and smiled. "Better."

He stroked a hand up and down my arms and kissed the top of my head. "Definitely."

"I don't want this," I whispered. "I don't want there to be more."

"We'll meet with him and verify your connection. Perhaps what you're feeling has more to do with recognizing a fellow hybrid."

"Then what does that say about us?" I asked and tilted my head back to look at him.

Smiling wide he said, "We are no longer based solely on a connection, are we?"

Heat bloomed across my cheeks. He was right that now,

after being with them for this long, it wasn't the connection alone that drew me to them. It was their personalities, their minds, bodies, their souls. The way they made me laugh. The way they made me feel.

"This is your life, Ember. It is up to you to decide what you want to do. Even if that means severing things with all of us and returning to being a hermit. We all want you to be happy, to live your life how you want."

Despite only knowing them a month, I knew leaving them wasn't an option.

"I don't want to be a hermit again. I want to help hybrids, end the H.E., and explore the world."

He leaned down, pressed his lips to mine, and whispered against my lips, "Then that's what I will help you do."

"Swear?" I asked.

Tracing an x over his heart, he nodded. "Swear."

"And you promise you're not mad at me?"

He kissed each of my cheeks before leaning back so our eyes could meet. "I promise I am not mad at you."

"But you didn't even say anything about my new dress," I teased.

Smiling, he sat up, helping me sit up as well, then waved at me. "Stand up. Do a spin."

"What?"

"Twirl. I want to see what it looks like as you twirl," he explained.

Feeling silly, but embracing it, I stood and twirled in a circle, smiling like a fool.

When I finished spinning, he was on his feet, and grabbed me by the hips. "You look beautiful and that dress is very pretty. I think we should test out how it looks on the floor." Sliding his fingers beneath each of the straps, he pushed them off my shoulders.

However, the dress wasn't held up by the straps, so they just fell down my arms and the dress stayed.

His frown caused me to burst into laughter.

"I've changed my mind. I don't like this dress. Take it off now."

As he reached for me, I ran around the couch, hands out. "Wait, let's talk about this."

He growled and prowled after me, eyes slightly glowing. "Don't you know you shouldn't run from a predator?"

"Only when you don't want to be devoured," I teased.

His eyes glowed brighter and he growled louder as he leapt over the couch.

Screeching, I turned and ran towards my bedroom.

I made it just inside the bedroom door before he tackled me onto the bed and started peppering my neck with kisses and nibbles.

"Caught you," he growled.

In a super sarcastic, high-pitched voice I said, "Oh no. Whatever shall I do now that I've been caught?"

He bit into my shoulder and I gasped, which quickly turned into a moan. "Perhaps I should tie you up for running," he rumbled against my shoulder.

My heart pounded faster at the thought of being tied up.

"Oh, do you like that idea?"

"No," I lied.

He sat up and smacked my butt. "No lying."

Looking over my shoulder I said, "I don't think spanking is the way to go to get me to *stop* doing something."

Smirking, he flipped me over, grabbed both of my wrists in one of his hands, and pinned them above my head on the bed. "Let's try this then." His other hand reached down, slid up my leg, and rubbed my clit.

My hips arched and I gasped, but he leaned his head down and bit my throat, which caused me to still.

His bite turned into kisses as his fingers moved quickly, building the pressure in my lower stomach. The next time he bit into the side of my neck, I orgasmed and screamed his name. Immediately, he plunged two of his fingers inside of me, pumping fast.

Just as I was about to orgasm again, he removed his fingers.

I whined and he chuckled against my check, beginning to pump his fingers in and out. Burying his fingers as deep as he could, he curved his fingers until they pushed against my g-spot and moved so quickly, that I barely had time to register my orgasm was building before I was screaming and plunging over the edge.

He growled softly. "That wasn't what I'd planned."

I arched a brow. "You weren't planning on making me orgasm?"

A smirk lifted up one side of his mouth and he said, "No, I'd planned on bringing you just to the edge until you begged me to forgive you for misbehaving and only then would I give you your release."

"Well, since your plan is already ruined ..." Jerking my

arms down, I pulled out of his hold, used my hips to flip us over, and scooted down to remove his pants.

"That was a nice flip," he praised as he lay on his back, put his hands behind his head, and smiled.

"It should be illegal to be so handsome," I said as I looked down at him, his biceps flexed and on display, and unadulterated confidence as he allowed me to take over.

Jerking his pants off, I freed his rock-hard erection. Leaning down, I took him into my mouth, swallowing down as much of him as I could.

He moaned and his hands fisted in the sheets of my bed on either side of him.

Pulling my hair back, I knelt between his legs, looked into his eyes, and slowly, as slowly as I dared, took him deeper and deeper into my mouth, relaxing my throat to allow him in.

His eyes stayed glued to mine as I continued the slow, but deep pace.

I blinked and suddenly I was on my back, dress pushed up above my hips, and he was pressed against my entrance, holding his upper body up on his hands.

"It's been too long," he said, his voice rumbling. Pressing forward just enough the tip of him slid inside. "Okay?"

I nodded vigorously. "Yes, please."

He smiled, dazzling me with it, and thrust his hips forward, burying his full length inside of me.

The stretch made me gasp and arch my hips up.

Leaning up, he grabbed my hands in one of his and pinned them above my head. "Be a good girl, stay still, and I'll give you what you want."

"Yes, alpha," I said, knowing he liked to hear that.

He thrust his hips forward as he moaned. "Good girl."

Before him, I never would have thought being ordered around or told I was a good girl would turn me on, but here I was, drenched as he held me and whispered praises while thrusting harder and faster.

"Come with me," he ordered me as his thrusts began to grow more frantic.

I nodded, not trusting my voice.

Releasing my hands, he gripped my hips, tilted them up, and shouted my name as I came and shouted his.

CHAPTER
FOUR

"Reasons being a rabbit shifter is a good thing," I read as I sat on the grass facing Silverowl.

He sat cross-legged, his hands folded in his lap, and a patient expression on his face that reminded me of a librarian.

When we'd first come out here for my shifting lesson, everyone had tried to stay, but he ordered everyone into the house. I had thanked him at least five times.

"Number one, I'll be cute."

He rolled his eyes.

"Number two, I'll be fast."

He nodded.

"Number three, better hearing, hopefully."

He nodded again.

"Number four, bunnies have cute tails."

He shook his head and chuckled.

"Number five, I could be bait to lead all the predators away."

He sighed.

"Number six, I'll be small, so I could hide or fit into smaller places. Number seven, in bunny form I'll eat less meat so it'll be cheaper to feed me."

"Okay," he said and shook his head, "I can see you are still having trouble accepting how it is beneficial, so let's get you to shift and then I'll talk you through them."

"I tried; I swear!" I protested.

"Deep breath, close your eyes, focus on your magic in your core."

Instead of trying to defend myself, I did what he said. My magic swirled within my core, ready to be used since I hadn't used any magic yet today, only trained in fighting.

"Picture a rabbit, envision it from the tip of its nose down to the tip of its tail. Hold that image in your mind, call upon your magic, and will your body to become the rabbit."

Become the rabbit. Become the rabbit.

I pictured a cute little white rabbit with an adorable pink nose twitching as it smelled the grass, fluffy white fur, and a bushy white round tail.

"Become the rabbit," I whispered and drew in a slow, deep breath as my magic swirled faster and spread throughout my body.

"Open your eyes, EmberRew," Silverowl whispered.

I opened my eyes, expecting to find myself in the same position, but instead found myself much lower than I had been. Lifting my hand, I blinked at the white fur-covered paw.

Rabbit's foot.

I was a rabbit!

A tiny, terrified squeak came out of my mouth.

"You're okay," Silverowl said. "You're in your rabbit form." He pulled out his cell phone and snapped a picture.

I opened my mouth to yell at him or growl or whatever rabbits could do.

He turned the phone around and showed me the picture.

My mouth snapped closed as I looked at the adorable white bunny, exactly as I had pictured, but with ruby red eyes.

Looking over my back, I wiggled my tail, feeling giddy at the little fluff ball moving.

"Try walking around, er hopping around," he instructed.

Hopping instead of walking was really awkward and I was even more thankful he'd sent the others away.

"Stop trying to figure out how to move and let your body do it for you. Let your natural instincts take over."

Right. I was supposed to be a rabbit.

Aiming for a spot across the yard, I let my mind go and only thought about wanting to be over there.

Wobbling at first, I started hopping easier and then faster and faster until I was zooming around the lawn, Silverowl watching with a smile.

Skidding to a stop in front of him, my heart pounded wildly. I jumped straight up into the air, shocked when I was able to reach his eye level.

"Yes, bunnies hop very high when they want. Now, are you ready for your next lesson? This one is much harder."

I bobbed my head up and down and hopped around in a circle.

"You're going to try to shift into warrior form," he explained.

Warrior form? I was a rabbit. How could I shift into a half-rabbit half-human form? Would I be like a tiny human?

"Warrior form for smaller shifters usually takes the best parts of the animal and combines them with your human parts. So, what are the best parts of your rabbit form? Your strong legs, your long ears, right?"

Okay. I could do this.

"Focus on your magic again, let it spread throughout your body, let it reshape you into the best form you can be."

Right. Rabbit legs, bunny ears, cute tail.

My magic spread throughout my body, building larger and larger, and I felt my form changing. More and more it spread, but the magic started to falter as I wondered what I looked like.

"Focus on the form you want to take," Silverowl said urgently. "Hold the image in your mind just like you did before.

I was trying!

Rabbit legs, ears, and a cute tail. Bushy white rabbit tail.

"Whoa," Silverowl whispered.

Opening my eyes, I looked down at my body. I was mostly human, but my hands were giant white bunny paws, my legs were shaped like a rabbit's and definitely at least twice as muscular as my human ones. Reaching up I felt long ears above my head and when I peeked over my shoulder, I smiled at the fluffy white tail. "I did it!" I shouted and hopped up and down.

Silverowl circled me, his eyes wide. "How very interesting. I've never seen a warrior form like this before."

"Did ... did I do it wrong?" I asked nervously and pressed my paws together.

He shook his head. "No, no there's nothing wrong. You're just so ... unique."

"Unique means weird," I said and put a paw on my hip.

He snapped another picture and showed it to me.

I gasped. "That's what I look like?"

He nodded.

"Whoa."

Taking his phone back, he put it in his pocket and said, "Try walking and running now."

With my differently shaped legs, it was slightly difficult to take normal steps, but I was able to after a moment. Running took even longer to figure out.

"Try jumping up, straight up," he instructed. "As high as you can."

Squatting down, I tensed my muscles, tilted my head back as I looked skyward, and jumped.

"Holy hybrids on a hill," Caleb gasped from below me.

I looked down and screamed. I was at least fifteen feet in the air. Flailing my arms, I tried to figure out how to land. My body shifted into my human form as I fell, which worried me even more. Would I break something if I landed now?

"I've got you," Caleb assured me as I fell, his arms out, ready to catch me.

As promised, he caught me, not even stumbling a single step forward as he did.

I panted, my heart hammering and magic feeling like it was depleted.

"That's enough for today," Silverowl said. "You did great."

"Thanks. Can you send me the pictures?"

"Pictures?" Caleb asked.

"Great job, EmberRew," Silverowl praised.

"Ember," I corrected.

He frowned. "Do you not like your elven name?"

Caleb set me down and I brushed down my shirt. "It's just ... I don't really want to keep a name my birth parents gave me when they didn't want to even keep me."

"Would you prefer I rename you?" he asked.

I blinked. "Huh?"

"As a prince of the elves, he can give you a new elven name," Caleb explained. "If you don't have family members who can change your name, a royal can in their place."

"Oh, um, maybe? I hadn't really thought about that since I didn't know it was possible."

"I'll send you my suggestion with the images and you can let me know what you decide," he said and patted my shoulder as he walked inside. "No pressure."

Did I want to change my name? EmberRew did fit what my animal form looked like.

"So, being a rabbit shifter isn't all bad?" Caleb asked.

"I can't believe I jumped so high," I said and shook my head while laughing.

"That warrior form looked incredible. We definitely want to have you train in that form as much as you can."

"Did you see me in my animal form?" I asked, eyes narrowed.

He shook his head. "I came outside when you jumped in your warrior form."

"Well, I'd try to show you my form, but I'm feeling pretty magically exhausted."

Draping an arm around my shoulders, he pulled me towards the house. "I'm not worried about it, I'm sure I'll see your other form soon."

"How do you know that?" I asked, leaning into his warmth.

"Once you shift, doing it again is much easier and you'll find you want to do it."

"Well, don't hold your breath," I teased.

"Welcome to being a shifter!" Fox yelled when I stepped inside.

"Thanks," I replied and returned his wide smile with my own.

"So, now your training is going to evolve even more," Rhys said. "Learning to fight in your animal and warrior forms are essential."

"Fighting in my animal form is not going to happen," I said with a laugh.

"Why not?" Triston asked from the couch where he was battling against Deryn on a fighting videogame.

"I'm tiny," I admitted.

"Change!" Caleb said. "Come on, I want to see your animal form."

"Nope. Didn't you just say you weren't worried about it?" Shaking my head, I ducked out from under his arm, and hurried out of the room and towards the kitchen to grab a snack and a bottle of water.

"Just once for a second!" he begged. "How small are we talking? Like this big?" He held his hands about basketball size apart.

Jolie turned around from the fridge, a bag of shredded cheese in one hand and a bag of tortillas in another.

"Oh, quesadilla! One for me, please," I requested and hopped up to sit on the counter.

"Come on, just once, please," Caleb begged, stuck out his bottom lip, and widened his eyes.

"Why are you using your puppy eyes on her?" Jolie asked.

Sighing, I crossed my arms over my chest. "He wants me to change."

"Were you able to?" She set the tortillas and cheese down and went back to the fridge to grab some leftover chicken from tacos they'd made the previous day.

"She turned into a human-sized rabbit and jumped like forty feet into the air," Caleb told her.

"I wasn't a human-sized rabbit. It was my warrior form," I corrected. A human-sized rabbit sounded absolutely terrifying. My phone pinged and I pulled it out to see the images from Silverowl.

Caleb tried to look over my phone, but I tucked it against my chest. He whined and shifted into a wolf, tucking his tail between his legs as he whined at me.

"Wow, that's just dirty," Jolie said and shook her head.

Hopping down, I showed her the images, but kept the phone tilted so Caleb couldn't see.

"Oh, wow. That is quite an interesting warrior form. How fast can you run in that form?"

"I didn't try running in that form yet. Those legs are more made for hopping and moving forward is ... difficult."

Caleb growled and bit my pant leg, tugging on it.

"He thinks you'll give in because he's being cute," Jolie said as she glared down at her son. "Worked on me a lot as he was growing up. Sorry."

Reaching down, I patted his head, then scratched behind his ears.

One leg started tapping against the floor as I found the spot right behind his ear he liked.

"Sadly for him, I'm used to adorable animals and it won't work on me."

"I'm impressed you learned so quickly," Jolie praised. "I can't wait to see what your warrior form is capable of."

"Mom, you're supposed to be on my side," Caleb pouted after shifting to his human form.

She scoffed. "Why would I be on your team? Have you forgotten that I know what it's like to be the only girl surrounded by men who always team up together? No, you've got your brothers to be on your side. I'm on her side."

"Thanks, Jolie," I said as warmth built within my chest. I knew she would have my back in a fight, but hearing her tell her son she was on my side, even a silly one like not wanting to shift, made me feel special.

"Now, stop teasing your girlfriend before you make her mad and then come crying to me to try to get help to fix what you messed up," she accused him. Stepping back she said, "And you know what else? You make us lunch."

He stepped up behind her and set his chin atop her head, dropping his shoulders down slightly to put more weight on her and asked, "Just you and Ember want a chicken quesadilla?"

She grabbed his arms and wrapped them around her so he hugged her. "Yes, please."

He squeezed her, then stepped to the side of her and started assembling them. "Okay, give me five minutes."

Jolie grabbed my hand, tugging me off the counter, and lead me out of the kitchen. When we were in the game room she turned and said, "And *that*, my lovely soon to be daughter-in-law, is how you convince one of your males to make you food so you can go play games while making them stop pestering you."

"You've got all the tricks, don't you?"

She laughed and shook her head. "Wait until you spend time with Leona. They aren't tricks, but those men are wrapped around her finger. She sneezes and one has a tissue, another has cold medicine, and the other two are helping her lie down on the couch while massaging her feet and neck."

"So, what game are we playing?" I asked.

"You choose. I've played them all a million times, so I like them all."

"Karting it is!" I shouted and ran to set it up.

CHAPTER
FIVE

"Date night?" I asked, blinking as my brain tried to comprehend what the guys had just told me after waking me from a nap.

"We want to take you out on a group date tonight, yes," Caleb said.

"We've been together, but not really spending time together," Triston said. "We want to do something together."

"And I've been away a lot recently," Branson added.

How could I say no now?

"Okay, how should I dress?" If we were doing this, I needed to know how to dress and get prepared to get ready.

"We want to leave in two hours, dress is formal," Triston answered.

"Formal? Like, one of my ballgowns, a club dress, or a summer dresses?" Clarification was important.

"Club dress," all three said simultaneously.

"What about Riddick?" I asked. He hadn't come with them to my apartment.

"He's finishing up some work for Mom, but he should be done in the next thirty minutes. He'll be joining us as well."

"Okay, you all need to leave right now so I can start getting ready," I ordered.

Their smiles, the excitement that they all permeated, was so worth it.

"Meet in the foyer in two hours," Caleb ordered me and all three hurried out of my apartment.

Running to the shower, I quickly scrubbed my hair and body, using the new non-scented items that Caleb had ordered me. Apparently, the ones I'd been using had messed with my scent and he didn't like them. Shifters were very particular about scents.

Once clean, I used the heated lamp over the shower to dry my body and a hair dryer with my body bent over and head upside down to dry my hair and make it fluffy simultaneously.

Once dry, I applied my makeup, then styled my hair better. Opening my closet, I pulled out the emerald green dress that Caleb had purchased when we were at the mall. He'd seen the dress on a mannequin when I'd been changing out of the red ballgown for the first event we'd gone to together and had purchased it secretly for me. He swore that one he saw it there was no way he could resist buying it so that one day I could wear it.

Since I hadn't had a chance to wear it yet, tonight seemed like the perfect opportunity. Plus, most of my other dresses weren't really suited for the club.

This emerald green dress was thigh length, had a halter top with a low cut front to show off my cleavage, and a low back so that my entire back was bare. I slipped on my black ballet shoes since it sounded like I might be on my feet a lot and I wasn't yet comfortable in heels, no matter how pretty they were.

My jewelry collection had grown exponentially since I met Jolie, but I was *not* complaining. Digging through it, I found something to match the dress, a set of large diamond earrings and a necklace, secured them, then ran to the elevator to meet the guys.

I was the last one to arrive to the foyer, so all four turned around when the elevator doors opened.

Triston whistled. Caleb smiled wide. Branson's eyes roved from head to toes and back again. Riddick's eyes darkened and he took a step forward, but stopped himself.

"Is this outfit okay?" I asked and spun in a circle in the middle of the foyer.

All four nodded simultaneously.

Branson wore a pair of black slacks that looked like they were about to split from his muscular legs. His shirt was a black with silver pinstripe long-sleeved button-up shirt.

Caleb wore tan slacks and a black short-sleeved button-up shirt with the top two buttons open, giving him more of a casual look.

Triston's outfit was similar to Branson's, but his shirt was black with a red stitched tiger on the back.

Riddick had grey pants and a long-sleeved white button-up shirt with the sleeves rolled up to his elbows, showing off his muscular forearms.

"You all look handsome," I breathed, trying to rein in my desire. Turning, I headed towards the door.

"Wait," Caleb said, grabbed my wrist, and pulled me back a step. "We got you something."

I turned, frowning. "You got me something?"

"A gift," Triston clarified.

Branson held out a small black rectangular box with a red bow on it. "We picked it out together."

"Aw, that's so sweet," I said, my smile wide as I took it and opened it. Inside of the black velvet box on crème-colored padding was a silver tennis bracelet with four little rubies hanging from the clasp, and a puffed silver heart. "Oh my gosh," I breathed, tears building in my eyes as I traced the four rubies. "This is ... gorgeous. I love it. Thank you."

Branson took it out and clipped it on my wrist. "We thought you might like a gift with something to indicate the three of us."

"And the heart has a tracking device inside of it," Caleb said proudly.

"If we didn't already have a connection that allowed you to track me, that would be a little creepy, Caleb." I shook my head as I laughed.

"It's actually a pretty common gift for those courting to give the woman," Riddick said. "Since part of courting is proving your ability to provide safety and protection."

"I'm more concerned with how you treat me emotionally than your ability to beat someone up." But it was pretty sexy to watch them fight to protect me.

Caleb's phone pinged and he glanced down to read a message. "Ezio is here, are you ready to go?"

Holding my arm up to look at the pretty new bracelet, I nodded.

Caleb took my hand and tucked it into his arm, patting it gently. "Then let's be on our way."

Triston pulled open the door with a bow.

Stepping outside, I was immediately blinded by a barrage of camera flashes and shouting.

Caleb slipped his arm around my waist and tugged me against his side, immediately making me feel safe. "Good evening," he said over the noise. "Can you please stop shouting and scaring Ember?"

The voices ceased and the camera flashes decreased tenfold.

"Thank you," he said. Glancing up, I saw him smiling for them, but it was tense. "Ms. Martin, you have a question?"

"Yes, we wanted to ask how you're adjusting to a relationship similar to your parents'?"

"There are trials and tribulations for every relationship, are there not?" he asked.

Several people chuckled.

"Can you tell us about yourself, miss Ember?" one of the people asked.

"Were you always interested in Prince Caleb? Did you travel here to try to catch his eye?"

"What's it like dating a prince?"

"Did you draw those creatures in hopes of attracting Prince Caleb's attention?"

The questions were shouted so quickly that I didn't even get a chance to draw a breath to answer before the next was asked.

"It seems you've all been misinformed," Caleb said sternly. "I found Ember while investigating a rogue mage near her home in West City. It was I who initiated our relationship, not her."

An older male with glasses holding a pen and paper while scowling asked, "And you two? Did you know Ember before? What do you think about having to share her with the prince?"

Triston stepped up next to me and said, "I don't have to do anything, sir. Branson and I chose this the same as Ember, Riddick, and Prince Caleb chose this. We are all consenting parties who want to pursue this pack and relationship to see if we might convince our lovely little Ember to stay with us the rest of her life." He looked down and winked at me, making me blush.

"If you'll excuse us, we're on our way to take this beautiful woman on a date. Thank you." Caleb tugged me forward and the reporters separated, but the camera flashes began again.

Ezio stood at the curb with a black SUV, doors opened and waiting for us. "All good?" he asked.

Caleb nodded. "Seems like someone is spreading rumors about how Ember and I met. Or they're just speculating and trying to fish information from us."

"You could just make a public announcement," Ezio suggested. He looked down at me and smiled. "You look lovely, Ember."

"Thanks, Ezio." I climbed into the SUV and buckled my seatbelt.

"Where to?" Ezio asked once everyone was inside and doors were shut.

"District Seven," Caleb answered.

District Seven was one of the most popular dance clubs in the city. There were always celebrities going there and royalty, like Caleb's uncles and cousins. I had never heard of him visiting it though. The only reason I even knew about the club was because they talked about it on the news often.

"Understood," Ezio said and started driving.

"You handled the reporters really well," I commented.

Caleb shrugged. "They were nearly a constant when I was growing up. My dads talked me through how to handle them when I was young. Plus, it helps to know they're just curious about our lives since they don't get to see much of it."

"I'll let you all handle talking to them," Branson grumbled.

"You're a shy one, huh?" Ezio asked. "Funny for a large guy."

"Not shy, just don't like answering questions about my personal life. It's none of their business why I'm in this pack or dating Ember."

"Did you decide about your name yet?" Caleb asked.

"Oh, what alternate name were you offered?" Triston asked. "You haven't told me yet."

"Rubyhare Ember Jasperwood was the new name Silverowl offered," I said. "I'm not sure what I want to do. Part of me wants to change it, but part of me also wonders if I should accept the name even if I don't want to accept anything from my birth parents." It wasn't that I didn't like Rubyhare as a name, I actually did like it a lot, but I just wasn't certain what I wanted yet.

"What did rew mean again?" Branson asked.

"It's a description of her rabbit form, red-eyed white furred," Caleb answered.

My eyes widened as I turned to look at him. "How did you know that?"

"I did a lot of searching for information on rabbits. Figured if I'm dating a rabbit shifter that it would be helpful to know more about you."

"We should make a shared document," Branson said. "So, we can all discuss and share the information."

Caleb nodded. "I'll create one and put it on our shared drive."

"You have a shared drive?" I asked.

"Now that we're on the same phone plan and part of a pack, we set up a shared drive to upload important information," Triston explained. "Much easier than emailing each other constantly."

Branson and Caleb nodded.

We pulled up to the club and as usual, there was a line wrapped down the block.

Ezio put the vehicle in park, walked around, and opened the door for us, his hand out to help me step down. "Big smile," he told me, giving me one himself. "You're going to go inside and have a ton of fun."

I put on a big smile, nodded, and accepted his hand out of the vehicle.

People murmured as they saw me, unsure of who I was.

The murmuring turned into screams as Caleb stepped out and smoothed his hands down his shirt. He took my hand from Ezio and interlocked our fingers. With a wink, he pulled me towards the entrance.

The bouncer immediately pulled the rope to the side, bowing as we walked inside.

Women called Caleb's name, trying to get his attention, but he ignored them all, eyes forward as we headed inside.

The doorman opened the door with a bow as well and I wondered if he hated them bowing or enjoyed it. I'd ask him later.

Inside music played loudly and a soft scent of cinnamon permeated the air.

A slim man with slicked back hair rushed to us and bowed. "Your Highness, your table is ready." He spun on his heel and lead us to the VIP section. The VIP section was four u-shaped black padded booths with large low circular tables in the middle. Each of the four was sectioned off by red ropes and the entire four were surrounded by guards and more ropes to prevent people from entering who weren't supposed to.

We sat in the third table, I scooted into the middle of the u-shape, Branson on my left. Caleb leaned over the ropes to shake hands with someone at the table beside ours.

"Nephew!" a voice shouted from the booth on the other side of ours and a head of curly hair popped up as he stood, pushing around his friends to get to the rope that separated us.

I knew immediately he was related to Rhys because he looked like a younger version of him.

"Hello, Uncle Gavin," Caleb replied and walked over to embrace him.

Gavin was Rhys's youngest brother, a big advocate of creating schools for all races to attend in the outlying rural areas. Everything I'd heard about him said he was a genuinely good person.

"What are you doing here? Did you bring Ember?" Gavin hopped over the rope, leaned around the booth so I could see him, and waved. "Hi! You must be Ember. I'm Gavin."

"It's nice to meet you, Prince Gavin," I replied with a smile.

He introduced himself to the others. "It's so cool to see your hybrid pack together. The power you guys are emanating is awesome."

"Emanating?" I asked.

"Uncle Gavin has a really strong sense for powers," Caleb explained.

"Is this your first time here?" Gavin asked.

We all nodded.

"Then let me buy your first round!" He raised his hand and waved at a woman in black shirt and pants I hadn't noticed standing nearby.

She hurried over and bowed. "Yes, Your Highness?"

"Can you please put this table's first round on my tab?" he requested.

She bowed her head again. "Certainly, Your Highness."

"Thank you, Uncle," Caleb said.

Gavin winked. "Keep 'em on their toes, Ember. Have a great night!" He returned to his side and I wondered what he meant about keeping them on their toes?

After placing our drink order, Caleb sat down, scooting in to sit beside me, and draped an arm behind me.

Riddick sat on his other side, immediately looking out over the crowded floor of people dancing.

"Is it always this packed?" I asked.

Caleb shrugged. "From what my uncle and cousins say, yes. That's part of why I don't usually come here."

"What do you mean?" I asked.

He looked down at me and said, "It opens up the possibility of attacks. Being in the middle of a crowd that big gives those who hate me many more chances to attack me."

I completely understood what it was like to be hated for what you were, just for what you were born as, but I couldn't fathom how much it had to hurt to have strangers constantly trying to kill you.

Caleb's head snapped to the side and I looked in the direction as well.

On the other side of the ropes and security stood the waiter from the brunch place.

CHAPTER
SIX

"That's him," I whispered. "The waiter I felt the spark, pull with."

Caleb tapped Riddick on the shoulder, but Riddick was already getting out of the booth and to his feet. Riddick walked over to one of the guards and said something while pointing to the guy.

Caleb scooted out of the booth and so did Triston, Branson, and I, so we all stood in front of the table.

The guards let the guy in and he walked towards us hesitantly. Stopping before Caleb, he bowed. "Your Majesty."

Majesty ... king. He was calling Caleb his king.

"Ember told us about you. I'm sorry I haven't come to find you yet. I had planned to call you tomorrow," Caleb said and held out his hand to shake his. "What's your name, hybrid?"

"I'm Ambrose," he said. His eyes darted to me and I felt that slight pull again.

"You feel something?" Riddick asked.

I nodded. "It's a slight pull, not as strong as the feeling with you four."

Ambrose took a step forward, closer to me, but his eyes darted to Caleb as if seeking permission.

Caleb didn't move, so Ambrose took the last step to stand before me.

"Hello, again," I said and smiled, but it was a bit shaky from nerves.

He held his hand out. "Hello, Ember. You look lovely tonight."

Reaching out with a trembling hand, I shook his. This time there was no spark and the pull wasn't stronger, in fact, it lessened.

Exhaling softly, I put on a real smile as I looked up at him. "It's nice to see you again." Yes, he was incredibly attractive, but I had enough sexy males to deal with in the four around me.

Caleb relaxed and clapped Ambrose on the back. "Would you like to sit with us?"

He shook his head, frowning a bit. "No, I just wanted to come introduce myself to you."

"Here's my card," Riddick said and held out a business card. "Let's meet Monday."

Ambrose nodded. "Okay." He looked at me one last time, frowning, and headed out into the crowd of dancers.

"While he may be disappointed, I have to admit I feel better knowing he's not a potential mate for you as well," Riddick said and brushed back his hair that had fallen forward.

"What?" I asked.

"He's definitely better looking than all of us. How could we have competed with that?" he said, smiling wide.

I rolled my eyes and laughed. "You're ridiculous. All of you are attractive and you all know it."

"We still like to hear it," Triston said and slipped his arms around my waist, dancing behind me.

Dancing with him, I felt a bit of the stress that had been on my shoulders dissolve and allowed me to enjoy more of the moment.

We drank and danced, laughing and just enjoying each other's company for hours. It was one of the first times I'd not talked, but just spent time basking in the connection that thrummed between us all.

I admitted defeat after the fourth hour, plopping down on the end of the booth to drink water and give my legs a break.

Caleb and Riddick were talking to Gavin about something, the three of them scowling.

Branson and Triston had their heads bent together on the other side of the booth from me.

It had definitely been a great night out. Just one for us to strengthen our bond, which truly did feel stronger.

A pulse of something magical had me turning to look out towards the dancefloor. Scanning the crowd, I searched for the source and my eyes landed on a white-haired man glaring directly at me.

His mouth moved quickly and as he raised his hand, I realized he was about to attack.

Up on my feet, I crossed my arms over my chest and tried to summon a shield.

The magic he created was bright red and it streaked across the room towards me.

Caleb stepped in front of me, hands out, and his shield surrounded the entire VIP section just as the magic reached the ropes.

The magic sizzled against the shield, but didn't deflect or disappear.

Caleb scowled and grunted.

Was the power so strong his shield couldn't defeat it?

The white-haired man walked towards us as everyone on the dancefloor screamed and tried to flee.

The guards advanced, some in werewolf warrior form and some with magic in their hands.

The white-haired man battled with them, but my eyes were on Caleb.

His brows were furrowed and sweat was beading on his head as he continued to keep the shield up. The red magic continued to sizzle against it.

"What do you need?" Riddick asked.

"I don't know. It's not a magic I've seen before," Caleb grunted.

Stepping forward, I set a hand on his shoulder, feeling a need to touch him. "Can we teleport away?"

"I'm not sure what the magic is. It might hurt the others here if we leave," he said and his lip twitched in a snarl.

Right, he was a prince, a king and he didn't want others to get hurt because he fled.

"Get Ember out of here," Caleb ordered Triston and Branson. "Go to someplace safe while we handle things here."

"No, I'm not leaving," I snapped and gripped his shoulder

tighter. "We're pack, we don't separate just to save one of us."

"You're what matters to us, Ember," Riddick said.

"No," I growled. Looking back, I realized the man had defeated the guards and was heading closer to us.

"Caleb, what do you want me to do?" Gavin asked.

"Flee," Caleb ordered him.

"Caleb," Gavin growled.

"He's after us, Uncle. Please, take your friends and the others and flee. Get as many to safety as you can. I don't know what this magic is."

Gavin growled, nodded, and started shouting for everyone in the VIP section to head towards the exits.

Caleb grunted and the shield wavered. "I'm going to have to drop the shield. We need to move out of the magic's way. Ready?"

We all nodded.

"Now!" he shouted, grabbed me, and jumped to the right.

The red magical ball hit the booth in the exact spot I'd been sitting. It exploded and then imploded, destroying the part of the booth and table.

Holy acorns, that would have definitely killed me.

Riddick and Branson in warrior forms fought against the white-haired man.

Caleb stood and ran his hands along my arms.

"I'm good, go," I ordered him as I regained my breath from getting the wind knocked out of me.

Triston shifted into his warrior form and stood between me and the battle. "He's obviously after you."

"I know," I whispered and straightened. Gathering my magic, I used my telekinesis to raise two of the tables, keeping them parallel to each other.

"What are you doing?" Triston asked, eyeing the tables.

"Protecting my pack and swatting an annoying fly," I growled and strode forward, heading towards the fight, the tables hovering high in the air before me.

The man noticed me and ducked around Branson's punch, running fast at me.

Apparently, he hadn't noticed the tables.

Slapping my palms together, I sent the tables at him from either side, crushing him between them.

He cried out and tried to get free, but I interlocked my fingers, keeping the tables crushing him. Only his head was above the tables and his feet dangled uselessly below them, but above the ground, kicking to try to find purchase.

"How dare you ruin my date night," I growled at him and pushed my palms harder against each other.

The tables creaked from the strain and the man cried out again.

"You must die," he yelled. "Death to all hybrids."

"Holy shit, Ember," Branson breathed.

"Are you part of the H.E.?" Caleb asked as he approached the man.

Ezio ran inside in his warrior form, spotted us, and ran over to stand beside Caleb. "Status?"

"Ember, how long can you hold this?" Riddick asked.

"Not much longer," I admitted.

The man smiled and said, "Your days are numbered, hybrid whore."

"No, your breaths are," Caleb snarled, pulled a sword out of thin air, and sliced his head off.

I dropped the tables and fell to my knees, panting.

Riddick picked me up and cradled me against his chest. "You did great, Ember."

"Riddick, I think I'm going to faint."

"It's okay, we've got you," he whispered.

My vision wavered and ears started ringing.

Caleb walked over to me and set his hand on my head. The ringing lessened and my vision straightened. "You used too much magic again," he chastised me.

"He pissed me off," I said softly and smiled at him. "And he tried to kill me so it only seemed fair I try to kill him back."

"Squishing him between tables was a smart move," Caleb said and nodded. "Since he couldn't use his hands, he couldn't create another spell."

"Let's get you all home," Ezio said. "This place is too exposed and we don't know if he came alone or not."

Caleb kissed the side of my head and nodded at Riddick. "Let's go."

We headed towards the front doors, but I said, "Put me down."

"Why?" Riddick asked. "You're weakened right now."

"There are going to be people out there taking pictures," I explained, "and I don't want H.E. to have the satisfaction of seeing me carried out, like they might have been successful. I want them to see pictures of us perfectly healthy so they know they failed."

Caleb smiled.

Riddick reluctantly set me down, but kept a hand on my lower back.

Once I was sure I could walk, I smoothed my dress and hair, and nodded. "Ready."

Caleb led the way with Riddick and I behind him. Triston walked on my other side while Branson brought up the rear, his large body providing full coverage of mine.

Cameras flashed and reporters called out questions, but we ignored them all, piling into the SUV.

The pictures and news articles the next day were exactly what I wanted. Us, confident and picture perfect exiting the club and not a single mention of H.E., only a crazed mage attacking us and being defeated.

I hoped my adoptive parents were fuming in whatever hole they were hiding in.

CHAPTER
SEVEN

Branson stayed with me the night after the dance club attack. Since he was so large, there wasn't enough room for anyone else, but they all seemed to want to leave me with Branson to give us time together, since he'd been gone a lot recently.

Waking up the next morning, drenched in sweat thanks to the burning hot bear shifter was not what I expected, though.

"Shower," I breathed as I swung the covers off.

He chuckled. "A little too hot, huh?"

I glanced behind me at the broad-shouldered, muscular man and licked my lips. "More than a little."

His smile widened and he climbed out of bed to follow me into the bathroom.

We both brushed our teeth first, then I turned on the shower and stripped out of my sweaty tank top and underwear.

One of his large hands slid around to rest on my stomach,

his palm as wide as my entire stomach, and he pulled me backwards, his erection against my back. "I've missed you, Ember."

I rubbed the forearm that was wrapped around me, tilted my head back, and looked up at him. "I've missed you, too, Branny Boy."

His lip twitched into a smirk, but it disappeared as he leaned down to kiss me. "Everything has changed so much."

Stepping out of his hold and into the shower, I nodded my agreement. "But it's also better, right?"

He joined me, letting the water drench him before he put a hand on either side of me, pinning me against the shower wall. He left a trail of kisses from my temple, down my cheek, to my jaw, and down my neck, to the shoulder where his mark was. "This is definitely better than pining for you and wondering if you felt the same."

Reaching forward, I gripped his erection and stroked him slowly. "Same," I breathed, my heart beating faster as he licked his mark and a shot of desire went through me.

One hand dropped from beside my head, palmed one of my breasts, and kneaded it before pulling back to squeeze my nipple.

I hissed in a breath and stroked him faster.

He moaned and dropped his hand down, nudging my legs wider apart, and then slid two fingers through my folds and into my wet core. "So wet," he moaned. "You want me, EmandEm?"

I nodded, bent forward and kissed his chest.

"How do you want me?" he asked and pumped his

fingers faster in and out of me then inserted a third finger, stretching me more.

"Against the wall."

"You want me to eat you or fuck you?" he asked, pulling his fingers out to rub circles around my aching clit.

"Both?" I replied.

He chuckled, dropped to his knees, kissed my stomach since that was where his head was level with, and leaned down to lick me.

I moaned and leaned my head back against the tile, the coolness a stunning opposite to the heat in my lower body.

Branson wrapped his hands around my hips, gripped my butt, and plunged his tongue into me.

"Yes!" I screamed.

Dropping his hands from my butt, he reached up with one to pinch and pull one of my nipples, the second hand dropped and he inserted two fingers into me while he licked my clit, his tongue swirling around and sucking.

His tongue and fingers matched pace and the faster his fingers and tongue moved, the quicker the pressure built before I screamed, grabbed his hair, and shattered.

My release dripped down my legs and his hand and he licked until my legs wobbled and I could barely keep myself up. Standing, he grabbed me by the butt, lifted me, pressed me against the tile, and pressed the tip of his erection against my entrance. "Was that good, Ember?"

I nodded, my heart pounding so fast it felt like a hummingbird's.

He pushed into me slowly, letting my body stretch and adjust to his girth. He held still once fully inside of me and looked into my eyes. "You are truly beautiful, Ember. I feel lucky to even exist in the same realm as you, but being connected to you, our bodies connected as one like this. There's no greater joy."

Tears sprung to my eyes, but they were quickly gone as he thrust in and out of me. I wrapped my arms around his neck, pulling myself forward to lick and kiss his neck.

He moaned and thrust harder and faster into me.

Nibbling my way down his neck to his collarbone, I sucked hard on one spot before resuming my nibbling.

Branson moaned, "Fuck," and thrust harder and deeper, making me orgasm in less than a dozen strokes.

Since he'd seemed to like it, I sucked on the same spot on his collar bone.

He roared my name as he thrust into me, but quickly pulled out as he came.

"Well, this was definitely a great morning so far," I breathed as he set me back on my feet.

We washed quickly and after I changed, we prepared to head to his apartment so he could dress and we could make breakfast.

Carrying his clothes, he walked down the hallway to the elevator with just a towel around his waist.

"Good thing it's only our pack that lives here," I joked.

He scoffed. "You think I'd be embarrassed walking out in public while everyone knew I'd just slept with a stunning woman like you?" He shook his head. "I may be private about things, but I am definitely not embarrassed."

He sadly got dressed when we got to his apartment, but

at least had on a tank top so I could ogle his arms and shoulders.

"How are you feeling about all this change?" I asked while I watched him scrambling eggs. I'd offered to help and he had declined, asking me to sit on a stool at the island instead. "You were going to go off and start your new life, your new plan, before he came back to help me.

"There hadn't really been a plan after I woke up at your cabin, honestly. Plus, the longer I spent with you, the more I didn't want to leave. I'd decided to leave because you ignored us trying to protect you and I thought you were confirming my belief that you weren't interested in me that way. Looking back, I realize that I had been keeping you at arm's length because I'd been scared to actually let you in or to get rejected by you. Kieran and I had left, but I'd hated being separated from you. The pain grew and then I sensed something was wrong and raced back as fast as I could." He sighed. "If I'd really thought about it and understood you just weren't used to depending on others and was doing the same thing as me, it would have helped, but hindsight is twenty-twenty, right?"

"And now?" I asked, staying completely still in case it might break the trance and he'd stop sharing.

"I can tell Caleb is our leader, our alpha. Being with this pack feels like I finally found the place I belong. Helping Dan and the werewolves solidifies that even more. This is where I'm supposed to be." He raised his eyes. "With them and with you."

"Even if that means dealing with reports and paparazzi?" I asked.

He sighed and shook his head in disgust. "Yes, even then." Setting the plate of scrambled eggs and bacon before me he said, "I'm pretty sure there's nothing you could do or ask of me that I would deny."

He sat on the barstool beside me, his plate of bacon and eggs twice as large as mine.

"So, I could steal a piece of your bacon and you wouldn't get mad?" I asked and reached towards one of the two strips he had.

He gently smacked my hand. "Don't get crazy, woman."

Laughing I leaned over and kissed his cheek. "Thank you for answering me."

He turned his head and kissed my lips. "Thank you for being with me."

We ate in silence and I felt a bit of pressure ease off my shoulders that I hadn't realized had been from my uncertainty on how he felt about me and the pack.

I helped him wash the dishes and then we cuddled on the couch and watched some television.

After the crazy previous night, it was nice to relax together. Yet, despite the relaxing time, I had a niggling feeling that things were about to get insane for all of us.

EIGHT

"Make sure you do your training while we're gone," Rhys ordered us.

"Don't skip your meals, either," Jolie ordered us. "It's important to eat healthy."

"We're adults, you do know that, right? We make our own meals all the time when we're away from here," Caleb said and arched a brow at his parents.

His mom and dads had been giving us reminders for five minutes as they stood beside the SUV they were taking to start their vacation.

"Give me a hug," Jolie ordered him and then waved me over to hug me next. "Stay together and protect each other, okay?"

I nodded. "We will."

"Call us if something happens, okay? I better not read about it first in a news article or see a news report on TV," Jolie ordered.

"We'll be fine, Mom," Caleb said and kissed her cheek. "Now get out of here and go on your vacation."

"Take lots of pictures!" I said as I backed up to stand beside Riddick.

They finally got into the SUV and headed on their way.

"I thought they'd never leave," Caleb breathed. "We better head out, too."

Ezio was off on a task somewhere else today, so he couldn't drive us. Instead, Declan had driven to pick us up since we were going to his place. "Do you need to get anything?" Declan asked.

"No," Caleb replied. "We're ready."

"Let's head out then!" Declan opened the side door and smiled at me. "Ladies first."

I pretended to pick up the side of a dress and skipped over to climb inside. "Such a gentleman."

"Uncle Declan is a lot of things, but gentleman isn't one of them," Caleb teased.

Declan scoffed. "Shows what you know about me."

"I guess we're about to find out, aren't we?" Caleb said.

Once everyone was inside, Declan started the drive through the city and to the outskirts where they had a house in the rural area.

Since Leona's mates consisted of multiple different races, they hadn't wanted to choose one of the clans' areas. And Leona said she preferred to be away from the city as much as she could.

I had a feeling it had something to do with her being a siren, but hadn't confirmed that yet.

"Leona's been counting down the days for you to come,"

Declan said and glanced at me in the rearview mirror. "She even bought new bedding and washed it twice just to make sure it wasn't scented for you guys."

"Aw, you guys didn't need to go to all that trouble," I said. "I was napping on my roof and in the woods, remember? A soft bed in a warm house is enough of a bonus for me."

"Ember's been counting down the days, too," Riddick said. "She bought a calendar just to mark off the days."

"Hey!" I shouted. "You're not supposed to rat me out."

All of them laughed.

"Is Silverowl going to be around much?" I asked.

"All of us took two days' vacation," he answered.

My mouth dropped. "What!" I screeched.

"When your mate is this excited about another pack coming over, you do whatever you can to ensure it goes smoothly and she's less stressed. For us, that meant taking the vacation days so we could all devote our full attention."

"We're not children that need to be babysat," Caleb grumbled.

"Oh, it has nothing to do with that, Caleb. It's that your aunt is excited to have another siren to train and to for all of us to offer you any advice or examples of how to navigate this type of relationship. Though, we know yours is different from ours since we didn't have a magical connection like you do."

"You're not connected?" Branson asked. "But still chose to share?"

Declan nodded. "My twin and I always knew we'd share a partner, but when Leona showed up in our lives with Thor and Silverowl dating her, too, we knew we had to adapt."

"Wasn't it hard?" Branson asked.

Declan nodded again. "Honestly, Thor was the one that needed convincing. The jealous wolf was in love with Leona first and it took some major emotional growth for him to accept and realize that he was going to join our pack."

Branson frowned and looked out his window. He said he was fine with our pack and the relationship, that it felt right, so why was he so curious? Was it because he couldn't fathom doing it without the magical connection? Why did that make my chest hurt to think about?

Triston draped his arm around my shoulders, and squeezed me against his side. "Stop spiraling in your thoughts, darling."

I didn't respond, but relaxed into his side and closed my eyes.

Riddick and Declan chatted from the front seat and Triston started purring softly. The vibration and sound made it easy to doze.

The vehicle being put into park woke me from my nap. I started awake and immediately felt the wetness on the side of my face. Looking over in shock, I saw I'd drooled on Triston's shoulder. "I'm sorry," I gasped and wiped at my face with the back of my hand.

He shrugged. "It'll dry."

My cheeks were on fire as we climbed out of the SUV, but the embarrassment was quickly forgotten as I looked at the adorable little cottage house with a white picket fence and various flowers planted along the fence line. "This is the most adorable house I have ever seen!" I gasped.

The front door flung open and Leona walked out wearing

a pretty pink and yellow summer dress. "Welcome to our home!"

Declan opened the gate and stepped to the side so we could enter.

I walked through and hugged Leona. "This is so cute! The flowers are gorgeous."

"That was Silverowl's doing," she said. "He is great with plants."

"Elven bloodlines," he said from behind her.

Leona released me and stepped to the side so I could see him.

"Is that why my little garden always flourished even in bad weather?" I asked, thinking back about the little plot I'd had.

He shrugged. "Most likely."

"Oh, it was one hundred percent your magic," Branson said.

I turned to look at him. "What?"

"All of the plants inside of your wards never died. As soon as you stepped outside of your wards, you could see the difference, especially in winter," he explained.

"But it snowed inside my wards," I reminded him.

"And the plants got buried under the snow, but never died. I dug one out to check."

How had I never noticed that before? I wished I had. I would have planted more things to sustain myself to avoid ever going back into town. Knowing it now, though, I would put some plants on the roof to grow herbs and things.

"Shall we go inside?" Leona suggested. "We have lunch ready."

"Oh, good. I am starving," Caleb said and kissed Leona's cheek as he walked by and into the house.

"That boy hasn't changed since he was born," she said and shook her head.

"Not true," Thor countered from inside the doorway. "He doesn't bite as much."

Caleb bared his teeth. "Don't be so sure."

Thor smiled. "I'll just pin you to the floor and smack your nose like I did when you were a pup."

"You could try," Caleb said and smiled back.

Thor tackled Caleb back out of the house and the two began wrestling around on the grass.

"That took longer than I expected," Kylan said as he came out to join us. "My bet was five minutes, but it only took two."

Caleb got out from Thor's hold and ran over, tackling Kylan. Declan smiled and jumped into the fray, so that it was Caleb versus Thor, Kylan, and Declan.

Leona put her arm around me and squeezed. "Welcome to the chaos, girl. This has been my life for about twenty years now."

"You don't look a day over twenty-four," Triston said and winked.

She giggled. "Okay, you're my new favorite. It's official."

We went into the house and she gave me a tour. I'd thought the house was small, but we found out there were two floors below ground, which allowed for more rooms and space. They even had a theater room.

"This is impressive," Branson said as he walked around

the bottom floor. "It doesn't even feel like you are underground."

Silverowl nodded. "We had to make sure it wouldn't since shapeshifters notoriously dislike being underground."

"You don't have a problem with it?" I asked.

"Although I can shapeshift because of my elven blood, I don't have the same senses or issues that the others do. One perk for us," he explained.

After showing us where our rooms were and moving our stuff inside, we went to the top floor, headed for the dining room to eat lunch.

Caleb had finally admitted defeat to his uncles, but all four were panting as they came inside. It was one of the first times I had seen Caleb so carefree.

"Did he visit you often?" I asked. "When he was younger."

Leona nodded. "Silverowl put a ton of wards around the property, our nearest neighbor on any side are at least two acres away, so it's pretty secure, which allowed him to play outside without too much worry."

"Plus, Leona was the only other siren, so he liked coming here for the lessons she gave him about controlling his emotions and avoiding affecting others," Silverowl added.

"Speaking of that, how is your training going?" Leona asked me.

"I've been able to lock my emotions up so it doesn't affect them even with our connection," I said proudly.

"What about shifting?" Silverowl asked.

I flinched. "I haven't shifted since our training."

He frowned. "Why not?"

"She's still embarrassed," Caleb answered, standing in the dining room doorway munching on a bread roll.

"Everyone, sit down and eat," Leona ordered.

We sat around the table and Declan and Kylan started setting out glasses. For Leona and I, they set flute glasses and everyone else had pint glasses. Declan opened a champagne bottle and poured it into Leona's glass, then mine and Kylan followed behind, pouring a splash of orange juice in them next. Finally, they poured beer from a pitcher into the pint glasses for the guys.

Before I could even reach for my plate, Triston and Riddick started putting food on it for me. I was about to get upset when I noticed Leona sitting back in her chair drinking from her glass with a smile as her mates did the same. She winked at me.

Oh, so this was a common thing? Reaching forward, I grabbed the flute glass and took a drink of the mimosa. "Delicious," I praised.

"It just takes some training to get your mates to understand the correct champagne to juice ratio," Kylan said with a smile.

Leona smiled. "Oh, and the training was just horrendous. Glass after glass of mimosas, adjusting the amounts until it is perfect. Just dreadful training."

"It sounds like it was quite the ordeal for you," I said to Leona.

She fake pouted and nodded. "It was."

Now that Leona and my plates were loaded, the men started making their own. We waited until everyone had food before we began eating. It seemed common for situations like this, with lots of shapeshifters, to not speak until after everyone had finished eating.

I didn't mind, the food was amazing, and I ate every last piece on my plate.

"Want more?" Riddick asked.

Shaking my head, I put a hand on my full stomach. "No, I can't possibly fit more right now."

"Then we'll wait a bit before we eat dessert," Thor said. "Let's go to the living room. It's more comfortable there."

Taking our drinks, we all went to the living room. Leona sat on a long couch, Silverowl on her right and Thor on her left. Kylan and Declan sat on either side of them.

The couch we took was smaller, so only Caleb, Riddick, and I could fit. Branson took the reclining chair and Triston sat on the floor, leaned back against my legs.

"I have an announcement now that we're all gathered," I said.

"Oh, exciting!" Leona gasped. "What could it be? Are you adding another to your harem? Running off to join the circus?"

"Auntie, shush," Caleb said with a chuckle.

She pouted, but then smiled at me. "Go on, I'm just teasing."

"I've decided to accept Silverowl's new name. If, you're still willing to rename me?"

Silverowl smiled so warmly that it caught me off guard, as the prince wasn't usually so expressive. "I'm so happy to hear that. Of course."

"What do we have to do to finalize it?" I asked.

"I just have to enter your name into our database. Your

current one isn't actually in there, since your parents were trying to hide you are a hybrid. So, I'll enter your new name when I return to my parents' house next week. I'll create a new birth certificate for you as well."

"You'll need to get a new ID card," Caleb said.

Silverowl nodded. "Yes, I'll have the paperwork ready for you after I enter it into our database. Welcome to the elves, Rubyhare Ember Jasperwood."

Tears built in my eyes and I quickly fanned my face. "I don't know why I'm crying." Fanning didn't help a few fell.

"Pretty sure any hybrid except Caleb would cry after a royal welcomed them to the clan," Riddick said.

Silverowl frowned. "You need an elven name as well, don't you, Riddick?"

Riddick's smile turned a bit sad. "My parents didn't want to give me one since it would expose what I was."

"How have we been brothers for this long and you never said anything?" Caleb growled. "Dad would have given you an elf name the first day you came to play if you had asked!"

"I didn't want to take advantage of our friendship," Riddick said with a shrug.

Leona laughed and shook her head. "You lot are so alike! Now I see the other issues you're running into. How old are all of you?"

"Twenty-eight," I said.

"Twenty-nine," Caleb answered. "Shouldn't you know that, Auntie?"

She rolled her eyes and ignored him, looking at the others.

"Twenty-nine," Riddick answered.

"Thirty," Branson said.

"You old man!" I gasped.

He growled, but it was clearly fake.

"Twenty-seven," Triston answered.

"Aw, the baby of the group," Leona teased. "Well, that makes sense. In your thirties is when you embrace more of yourself and stop having as much self-consciousness. Don't get me wrong, even at ..." she paused "... thirty-nine, I still have it."

Thor choked on his beer and started coughing loudly.

She turned to glare at him.

"Sorry, you're right, not a day over thirty-nine," he choked and cleared his throat.

"The point is, after interacting with you all, we've noticed a few things that we know will get better the longer you're together and the older you get. Like Caleb's jealousy."

"What? I'm not jealous," Caleb argued.

"You made her think you were mad at her because you thought another guy might also be connected to her," Leona reminded him.

He flinched and side-eyed me. "You told her?"

"I talk to her about a lot of things," I said while examining my drink, which was almost empty. That made me frown.

Triston looked over his shoulder at me, stood, grabbed my glass, took Leona's empty glass as well, and walked out of the room.

"He's definitely my favorite," Leona said which earned growls from Thor and Caleb. "See!" she shouted.

"How do we fix the self-conscious issues?" Branson asked.

She smiled softly. "Have you all considered therapy? Individual and couples?"

That had us all blinking.

"We can recommend ours to you. She's fantastic and really helped us out," Thor said.

"You go to therapy?" Caleb asked him.

Thor scowled. "Yes, I do. It's helped a lot, actually. You definitely need some therapy."

Caleb frowned, but didn't say anything back.

"We would love your recommendation," I said.

Triston returned with our drinks and I took a sip, mouth puckering a bit at the severe lack of orange juice.

"A tad more orange juice next time," Leona instructed him.

He nodded, left, grabbed more orange juice to add to our drinks, put the juice away, and sat down. "Understood."

"I do love a trainable man," she crooned.

Thor shook his head.

"So, can we see your animal form now?" Kylan asked with a wide smile.

With a sigh, I nodded. "Okay. Fine."

"Yes!" Caleb shouted and stood.

CHAPTER
NINE

"Just ... here?" I asked, looking around the living room.

"You are very small," Silverowl reminded me. "Not like if Kylan or Declan needed to shift."

"We can go somewhere else if you'd prefer," Kylan offered.

"No, it's fine," I conceded, took another drink of my mimosa, and set the glass down.

"Remember, just envision your form and let the change happen naturally," Silverowl said softly.

I nodded, walked over by the television where I had a bit more room, and closed my eyes. Picturing the adorable little bunny that I turned into, I felt the change immediately. This time was much easier than the first time.

"Oh, my god you are the most adorable thing I have ever seen in my entire life," Leona screeched.

Opening my eyes, I found the coffee table and everyone so much taller than when I'd been human. It was a little terrifying, but I took a slow, deep breath and reminded myself they were all friends.

Hopping forward, I went to Leona who bent and picked me up, setting me in her lap.

"Your fur is so soft! Oh, Rubyhare, you are absolutely perfect. How could you be embarrassed about this form?"

"You're perfectly snack sized," Caleb said with a wicked smile.

I spun and glared at him.

"Oh, that glare is even more adorable," Riddick said with a stupid smile.

"Ignore them," Silverowl ordered me.

I hopped in a circle to face him.

"Your shift was good this time, much better than your first, but it still took too long. You need to be able to do it instantaneously in case of emergency," he said.

"This size, she could be in a battle and sneak away between everyone's legs without them even realizing," Thor commented. "It would give you the perfect chance to get behind them and attack from there in your hybrid form."

"Yes, let's try that form next," Silverowl said. He held out his hands, cupped together. "Can I carry you outside?"

Leona scooped me up as she stood. "No, I'll carry her." She gently cradled me in her arms, smiling at me as she walked into their backyard. "You really are super cute. I love it."

Once in the backyard, she gently lowered her hands and I hopped out of them onto the grass.

"Wait!" Caleb shouted and ran out. He squatted down in front of me and ran his hand from the top of my head to my butt a few times. "You really are perfectly adorable, Ember. I just want you to know that. We all love you in this form."

Branson dropped to a squat next to Caleb and held his hand out. I hopped forward and rubbed my cheek along it. "He's right. I didn't think I could possibly find you more adorable, but here we are."

Their words did make me feel better.

"Okay, step back and let her shift into warrior form," Silverowl ordered them. To me he said, "Remember what your warrior form looked like and how it felt."

I bobbed my head, hopped a bit away from the guys, and closed my eyes. My magic gathered and spread throughout my body. After a pause, I felt it shift.

"Hot damn," Triston breathed. "That's amazing."

I opened my eyes and everyone started circling around me, inspecting my new form. "I still need to learn how to move properly in this form. The legs are a lot different than my human ones."

Silverowl nodded. "You definitely need to learn to run or hop fast as soon as possible. Actually, why don't you start now?"

"Caleb, let's work on your dragon-wolf warrior form," Kylan ordered him.

"Riddick, have you tried to turn into a dragon since your connection with Ember?" Declan asked.

While the guys got instructions and training from the others, I tried to walk and I could, but when I tried to jog, it didn't quite work. Switching to hopping, I tried that to move faster and found I could do a walk hop faster and faster until I was running quickly that way.

"Combining your movements definitely makes sense," Silverowl nodded. "Well done."

I preened at his praise. "Thanks."

"How high can you jump side to side?" Leona asked.

The first attempt to jump sideways was an utter fail, but after a bit, I was finally able to do it, though rather slowly.

"Practice that until you can do it easily," Silverowl ordered. "Also, practice hopping up and spinning around at the same time. The quicker you learn that, the quicker you'll be able to protect your back."

We spent two hours training before I collapsed on the grass, exhausted, and in my human form.

"Your homework this week is to shift into your rabbit form as often as possible," Silverowl said. "I want it to be second nature."

I raised my hand and gave him a thumbs-up. "Yes, sir."

"Shall we go inside, let you all shower, and then play some games?" Leona suggested. "We have several fun card and board games."

"More mimosas?" I asked as I sat up.

She rolled her eyes. "Duh."

I got to my feet, staggering a bit, but Caleb caught me and helped me straighten. "You definitely need to work on your stamina."

"That's what she said," I teased as I headed towards the house.

He scoffed. "Not to me, she didn't."

"How do you fit through the door with an ego that size?" Declan teased.

"Same way Uncle Thor does," he replied with a smirk.

Thor growled and tried to grab Caleb, but Caleb pushed Riddick between them and darted to the side.

"I will never not be envious of how much energy they all have," Leona said and shook her head. "Go on, go shower."

Since I wanted to play games, I took the quickest shower I could, and hurried to the living room where everyone was gathered, new drinks made and waiting.

"We're going to play this one first," Leona said. "It requires good teamwork and memory."

"Which is why the drinks will flow faster and stronger," Thor added.

After explaining the game, we let Leona's team go first so we could see an example. It was relatively easy to understand, but winning turned out to be hard, especially when you were laughing too much to answer.

After a few rounds of that game, we switched to another one. This one wasn't a team game, so we were all trying to beat each other. Turned out there were still teams as Kylan and Declan and Riddick and Caleb teamed up on people.

"Cheaters!" I accused. "You're working together."

Leona shook her head. "The twins always cheat and Caleb and Riddick might as well be twins at this point. They just think too much alike."

After another round, Leona caught my eye and winked, which I took as permission to start working with her. Together we ended up defeating all of the guys, and in the end fighting against each other for first place.

She won, but it was one of the best nights I had had.

"These are really fun," I said as I rubbed my stomach, sore from laughing so much.

"We'll have to buy them for the apartment," Triston said. "So we can play together."

I nodded. "Yes, please."

"Auntie, can we play the dance game now?" Caleb asked.

"Dance game?" I asked.

Leona laughed softly. "Fine! I know it's your favorite only because you always win."

"He doesn't always win, I've beaten him twice," Thor countered.

"Twice in twenty years," Caleb said.

"I think I'll play this time," Silverowl said.

Leona and her other mates looked at him with wide eyes.

"Really?" she asked.

He nodded. "It's a rhythm game, so I don't think it'll be that hard. Plus, you all seem to have so much fun when you're playing it."

"Great!" Caleb said and walked to the TV to set it up. "Another person I can defeat."

I rolled my eyes. "I've never played it, so don't count me out yet."

Twenty minutes later, it was obvious I was not going to win the game. Caleb and Silverowl were going back and forth for highest scores on songs, until Silverowl had a perfect run where he didn't miss a single note and even got bonus points for how well he did the dancing moves.

Leona whistled and cheered loudly, which made Silverowl smile wider.

"I concede," I said and collapsed on the couch. "I think I need to call it a night."

"Aw, you party pooper," Leona teased and immediately

yawned.

We all laughed.

"Come on, let's get you to bed. We've got a lot of training tomorrow," Caleb said and took my hand, pulling me to my feet.

"More training?" I groaned.

"Always training," Thor said. "Even we train every day."

"Don't worry, we'll have a big, yummy breakfast waiting for you when you wake up," Leona promised. "Night!"

Once in my room, I cuddled under my blankets, still smiling happily.

"Can I join you?" Riddick asked from the doorway.

"Sure," I agreed and patted the bed beside me.

He climbed in under the blankets and wrapped me in a tight hug. "Thanks."

My body relaxed, and I realized I hadn't been as relaxed in bed as I had thought.

Someone climbed in behind me and kissed the back of my head as they spooned me. "Good night, little bunny queen," Caleb whispered.

"Good night, my king."

He groaned and nipped my ear. "No teasing. We need sleep."

I chuckled. "Sorry."

"You did really well today," Riddick praised. "I don't think it'll be long before we can head out again."

Caleb nodded against my head. "Agreed."

"Thank you," I whispered, feeling immense pride at their compliments.

I could not wait for our next adventure.

CHAPTER
TEN

After an intense training session for all of us, an incredibly filling breakfast, and a hot shower that took longer than planned due to Caleb joining me, we all sat in the backyard soaking up some sun.

Riddick lay in his cheetah form to my left, purring with his eyes closed and the tip of his tail flicking up and down slowly. Branson was in his bear form on my right, snoring softly. Triston was in his tiger form sleeping behind me, purring as well, and allowing me to use him as a pillow. Caleb lay in his wolf form, head rested on my lap.

The sun on my skin, the deep, rumbling purrs, and being surrounded by the four made for a perfect nap.

"This is a great time for your next lesson," Silverowl said softly.

I cracked open one eye. "What?"

"Spend time with them in their animal forms and you in yours," he said.

Logically, I knew they wouldn't hurt me, but the thought

of being a rabbit with the four animals had my heart pounding.

"You'll be fine. They retain their minds in animal form and you still smell like you in rabbit form."

"We'll be right here if anything happens and we need to intercede, too," Kylan said.

"It's the safest time for you to do it," Declan added.

"If I get eaten, I'll never forgive you," I said to both my pack and Leona's.

After a shuddering breath, I closed my eyes and pictured my rabbit form. The change happened quickly and easily, but when I opened my eyes and found myself being stared at by a bear, cheetah, tiger, and wolf, my heart almost exploded in my chest.

Triston leaned closer and sniffed my fur, ruffling it with his large breath.

I held perfectly still, terrified of what he would do next.

His mouth opened and I clenched my eyes closed, but instead of biting me, he licked me.

A small, startled squeak came out of me.

Caleb crawled forward on his stomach, keeping his body as low as he could and rested his nose in front of me.

When I realized he wanted *me* to approach *him*, I leaned forward and sniffed his nose.

He sneezed and I tumbled head over tail backwards from the force of it.

Thor laughed, but it was cut off by a grunt.

My tumbling had sent me into Branson's side and he scooped me up in one of his giant bear paws, rolled onto his back, and set me on his huge, thickly furred belly.

He was so large I didn't know which way was which until he raised his head so he could look at me. He winked and dropped his head back down.

Hopping across his belly, I moved up to his chest.

As I was circling to lay down, Riddick walked over, bumped me with his nose, and licked me, his large tiger tongue licking half of my body in one swipe.

Yuck.

"That went better than I thought it would," Thor whispered.

Hopping onto Riddick's head, I stood on my back legs to glare at Thor, Declan, Kylan, and Silverowl.

"See, you were worried for nothing," Silverowl said.

"You know we'd never hurt you, Ember," Caleb said mentally.

"I wasn't sure if your instincts to protect me would trump your instincts to eat me," I replied.

He shot up to his feet. *"You can talk to us!"*

"Uh, I guess so." That was definitely a new development and would come in really handy, I bet, in the future.

"What's wrong, Caleb?" Declan asked, seeing him on his feet, facing Riddick and I.

Caleb shifted to his human form and said, "She can communicate telepathically with us in her animal form if we're in animal form."

All eyes swung to me.

"That's awesome," Triston said.

"Thanks," I said, feeling embarrassed and proud simultaneously.

"*Can you hear our thoughts or just when we want to speak to you?*" Riddick asked.

"*I think just when you speak to me because that sentence is the first I've heard from you,*" I answered.

I hopped off Riddick's head and headed away from the house, enjoying the movements of this body.

"*Want to race?*" Triston asked as he walked towards me, his long, striped tail swishing behind him.

"*You're definitely faster than me in this form,*" I said, but then nodded. "*Okay.*"

"*Ready. Set Go!*" he shouted and started running.

I hopped as fast as I could in the same direction he ran, my hop becoming gallop-like, but there was no contest on speed. "*You win,*" I gasped.

Riddick chuckled. "*Were you trying to race him?*"

"*You race him, Mister Cheetah.*"

"*Okay. Tell him,*" Riddick said and crouched like he was going to take off.

"*Riddick wants to race you,*" I told Triston.

Triston made a weird barking sound and lined up beside Riddick.

"*Ready. Set Go!*" I yelled to both of them.

They shot off across the grass, but they were too fast and I was too short to tell who won.

As they jogged back to me, they bumped into each other's shoulders, jostling the other in a teasing way.

I shifted into my warrior form and said, "Let's race again."

They lined up on either side of me, I squatted down, putting my fingertips on the ground and getting into a runner's position.

"Ready. Set go!" I shouted and pushed off with as much force as I could. My first hop sent me ahead of them and combining a human-style run with powerful hops forward kept me neck and neck with Riddick as we flew across the grass. I skid to a stop and slid, my feet going out from under me and fell on my butt. "Ouch," I hissed and started laughing as I lay onto my back. "That was fun."

"Wow, you're fast in that form," Riddick said as he reached a hand down to help me up.

I let him pull me to my feet and dusted myself off. "Still not faster than you."

"I think once you get even more used to this body you will be."

We walked side by side back to the house and rejoined everyone. Riddick shifted back into his cheetah form and lay in the spot he'd been before we raced.

"Caleb! Your phone is ringing off the hook," Leona shouted from inside the house.

Caleb sighed and walked inside. "Thanks."

I sat on the ground and pet Triston's head, running my hand between his ears across the top. He purred louder.

"Riddick, we've got to go!" Caleb shouted and ran outside with his phone in his hand.

"What's going on?" I asked.

"Ambrose is in trouble," Caleb answered. "We're going to go rescue him."

Everyone shifted to their human forms and stood.

"In the city?" I asked.

Caleb nodded. "The downtown park."

"Let's go," I said and headed through the house towards the front drive.

"No, just Riddick and I," Caleb said.

"What? Why?" Spinning around, I stared at him in disbelief.

"I think it's a trap," Caleb answered.

"All the more reason for you to not go with just the two of you," I countered.

"We'll all go," Leona said. "The more of us, the better."

"Auntie, you can't fight," Caleb said softly.

She glared at him. "I know you did not just tell me that I can't fight. I am a siren, one of the most powerful sirens to be alive right now. Everyone, get in the cars." She shook her head and mumbled, "Impertinent brat."

Caleb growled, but with no time to waste, we got into two SUVs, one with Declan driving and one with Kylan driving, and headed into town.

Thankfully, we were close enough and the twins were crazy enough drivers that it didn't take long to get to the park.

Once out of the vehicles, we spread out and headed into the park towards the sounds of yelling.

"I'm going to get an aerial view," Triston said and shifted into his dragon form, flying up into the sky.

"Stay with me, Em," Branson ordered me.

We spotted a huge group of people gathered and in the center was Ambrose fighting against half a dozen men.

Triston dropped down out of the sky and punched one of the attackers, knocking him away from Ambrose.

Caleb shifted into his warrior form, a combination of all of the forms, and ran into the fray. Riddick right beside him.

"Stay with Leona," Branson ordered me, shifted into his warrior form, and roared, scaring people out of the way so he could charge in as well.

Leona and Silverowl stood beside me with Thor behind us.

Declan and Kylan joined the fight and soon it was over.

"Something seems off," I whispered and looked around the crowd that had been watching.

"I can sense malice," Leona whispered. "From multiple people in the crowd. Like a lot of them."

The gathered group suddenly surged forward, closing around the guys and fighting them. The people directly in front of us turned around, shifted into wolf and dragon warrior forms.

Silverowl pulled roots from the ground and began binding people in them, holding them on the ground.

Thor jumped in front of Leona, attacking those nearest.

Leona sighed and shook her head. "Plug your ears, Ember."

Shoving my fingers in my ears, I watched her mouth open.

As soon as she started singing, everyone stumbled, and then fell to the ground.

Removing my fingers from my ears, I copied Silverowl and bound the now sleeping enemies in roots.

Walking over the sleeping people, I made my way to the center where only Caleb was standing. "Are you okay?" I asked, seeing blood on his arms and face.

He nodded, panting. "I told you it was a trap."

We quickly woke our people.

"Everyone okay?" Dan asked as he and several were-wolves ran into the park.

"Papa, what are you doing here?" Caleb asked.

"We saw the fight on the news, so we came to help, but Leona ended up just before we made it," he answered. He winked at her. "Nicely done."

She beamed. "Thanks."

"Take them for questioning," Dan ordered the were-wolves with him. "I have a feeling they're part of that nasty organization we've been trying to take down. Let's see if we can get any information out of them."

"Let me know what you find," Caleb said.

Dan nodded.

"What happened?" Ambrose asked, his hand to his head as he started to stand.

"Sorry about that," Leona apologized. "I didn't want to hurt anyone so the easiest way to end the battle was to make you all fall asleep. The grogginess will go away quickly now that you're awake."

"Who started the fight with you?" Caleb asked Ambrose.

Ambrose pointed at one of the guys on the ground beside them. "He attacked me as I was walking home from work through here and his cronies chased me. I'm glad I was able to get ahold of you. Thank you for coming."

"You need any healing?" I asked.

He shook his head. "The minor injuries I have will be healed shortly."

With the people getting put in proper restraints and all

our people awake and safe, I made my way out of the crowd, stepping over people until I was in an open spot.

Sitting down cross-legged, I watched everyone and waited. It felt good to have saved Ambrose and to capture two dozen of the people who were hybrid haters.

"Ember!" Caleb shouted.

I frowned. Why was he yelling at me? I was just sitting and waiting.

He and everyone shifted and turned towards me, their eyes wide.

Realization that there must be someone behind me finally hit and I turned around.

A large fist flew at my face.

On instinct, I shifted into my rabbit form, shrinking down so his punch missed me, and hopped to the side.

"What the—" The man shouted as he stumbled forward, thrown off balance.

Behind him were two more men and they dove for me, trying to grab me.

Not today! I was not getting kidnapped. Nope! Nope!

Hopping and dodging them as fast as I could, I made my way towards the others. Unfortunately, with my distraction, I had released eight of the enemies that had been held to the ground by my vines, so they were fighting again, too.

One of the men grabbed me by the scruff and snarled, "Got her!"

Shifting into my warrior form, I kicked him in the stomach as hard as I could, sending him flying backwards into both of his friends.

"Ha!" I shouted, but my victory was short-lived as a woman hit me with a bolt of lightning.

Screaming, I dropped to my knees, my entire body twitching.

Branson backhanded the woman, sending her flying into a tree with a sickening crunch. He ran over and stood between me and the men who'd been attacking me. "Can you stand?" he asked, his voice deeper and rumbly in his warrior form.

"I think so," I breathed as the pain lessened and the twitching decreased. Slowly, I got to my feet and wobbled a bit.

Caleb set a hand on my back as he walked by. "Good job, Ember." He continued past us, facing the three men who were snarling and growling at us. "Why are you trying to take her? What do you want with Ember?"

"Shut up, hybrid monstrosity," one of the men snapped.

"We don't answer to you," one of the others said.

Caleb straightened. "No? Well, you do answer to him." He jerked his thumb behind him and I realized Dan was beside me.

Dan growled and in a commanding voice ordered the men, "Sit!"

All three men dropped to their butts, eyes on the ground, and chests heaving.

"You dare attack my grandson's packmate?" Dan snarled. "You dare join an organization bent on destroying my beloved grandson? You shall be stripped of your wolves! You are banished from the pack, a rogue!" Reaching forward, he set his hand on the head of one of the men who immediately screamed.

"No! Don't! Please!" the man screamed and tried to move, but Dan's power held him in place.

One by one Dan went down the line, touching their heads and making them scream.

"What is he doing?" I asked Branson softly.

"Sealing their ability to shift, preventing them from turning into wolves," Branson whispered. "I'd heard they could do that, but that's absolutely terrifying."

"Good thing we're on his side," I whispered.

Caleb took my hand and pulled me into a hug, kissing the top of my head. "Let's go."

I nodded and wrapped my arms around him. "Okay."

"It's not over," one of the men panted as they were put in restraints. "They won't stop until you're dead."

"Then you better buckle up for a long ride," Caleb said. "Because I'm going to find every last one of you and destroy you."

CHAPTER
ELEVEN

"What would you like for dinner?" Triston asked as he stroked his fingers up and down my arm.

We lay in his bed in his apartment, smiling and content after an afternoon of vigorous and sweaty fun.

"Pasta," I said, my fingers tracing random patterns on his chest while my head lay on his bicep. "Some type of chicken and pasta meal."

"I think that can be arranged," he said and reached for his phone on the bedside table.

It had been two days since the attack with Ambrose and I'd spent all of that time dividing my attention between the four men. I wasn't sure what it was, but something about the attack had made me want to ensure I divided my time evenly between them.

"The others said that sounds good, too," Triston said. "Branson and Riddick are going to order some things from the grocery store. Do you want anything else from there?"

"Chocolate," I answered immediately. "Those chocolate

and vanilla ice cream cones Riddick had last time." They were really delicious.

He typed out the request and set his phone down, rolling onto his side to look at me. He brushed back my hair and said, "You're very beautiful."

"Thank you." I reached up and ran my fingers through his sandy-colored hair with streaks of black that reminded me of his tiger form. "Your hair is beautiful. I love the black streaks."

"We should probably get dressed," he said and kissed my forehead. "The others will be ready soon."

"I suppose," I said with a dramatic sigh.

"You could stay naked, I don't think the others would complain," he teased as he climbed out of bed and started dressing.

"Pretty sure there wouldn't be much cooking going on if I did that," I said with a chuckle.

"Oh, we'd be cooking alright," he replied making me chuckle.

That was one of the things I loved about Triston, he was funny and always made me laugh.

After getting dressed, I finger combed my hair and walked out to his kitchen, taking out vegetables for a salad. Triston pulled out frozen chicken breasts so they could defrost for dinner.

"Do you want to play a card game after dinner?" I asked.

Triston shrugged. "Whatever you want to do. Sounds fun to me."

"What would you like to do? I feel like you guys are

always asking me what I want and not doing what you want."

"We like doing the things you want to do," he replied and washed his hands before helping me chop vegetables. "It makes us happy to see you happy."

"Isn't the point of courting or dating to see what both sides enjoy, to help you make your decision on whether you want to be together the rest of your lives? What if you find out you don't have things in common and don't have a shared interest?"

"We all have a shared interest in videogames and card games. We have plenty of things in common."

"Like?" I probed.

"Being hybrids. Wanting to protect other hybrids and end the hatred against us."

"What else makes us a good unit?" I thought we were a good group, but sometimes I liked to hear their points of view on things. After being around Leona's group, it was obvious to me now that this was the pack I wanted, the mates I wanted, but we hadn't been together long enough for me to voice that. Plus, I had a niggling worry that something awful was headed our way that would test our connection.

Triston chopped carrots as he answered. "We vibe well together. All of us have different personalities, but together we're like a completed puzzle. Branson's quiet counteracts Caleb's boisterousness. Riddick's anxiousness is countered by my calmness."

That was very true. They balanced each other well and

having all of them around me helped balance my hectic mind.

Someone knocked on the door, so I set my knife down, walked over, and looked through the peephole. Caleb's blue eye stared back at me, startling me.

"You brat," I grumbled as I opened the door for him.

He kissed my cheek with a wide smile as he came in carrying a grocery bag. "Hello, beautiful."

"You got groceries delivered already?" I asked, shocked. They'd just asked for items less than ten minutes ago.

"These are snacks I already had," he explained. "Was easier to carry them in the bag."

I followed him to the living room to watch what he pulled out of the bag to set on the coffee table. Four bags of chips and a six-pack of beer.

He handed me a beer, grabbed one for himself, and another he carried over to Triston. "Cheers," he said as he tapped his can against Triston's.

I tapped mine against theirs and we opened them and took a sip.

"Do you need any help?" he asked Triston.

Triston shook his head. "I'm almost done."

Unlike Branson's and my place, Triston didn't have stools to sit at the island. Instead, Caleb grabbed two of the dining table chairs and turned them around to face the island. I sat on one while he sat on the other.

"My mom called and yelled at me about the park fight," Caleb told us. "I forgot to call her afterwards to let her know what happened."

"Whoops," I said and chuckled, able to picture exactly

how mad she would have been and what she would have said.

He took a drink of his beer. "My dads also gave me grief for not having at least one of us stay with you."

"Hey, I protected myself just fine."

"They said to tell you they were impressed with your shifting abilities and proud of how quickly you used them to defend yourself. Especially your warrior form."

I was pretty proud of myself, but hearing that they thought that made me even happier.

"Mom also said she was proud of you and that she's going to bring you back a souvenir."

"That's sweet," I said. "I've never been given a souvenir before."

Triston stopped mid-chop and raised his eyes to mine. "What?"

"Hermit, remember?" I said and chuckled.

"Speaking of you being a hermit, do you want to go on a day trip tomorrow?" Caleb asked.

I nodded immediately and shouted, "Yes!"

"Where are we going?" Triston asked as he put the chopped vegetables together into a large bowl.

"I figured since we're on the tail end of summer that it would be good to go to the beach before it started cooling down. Have you ever been to the beach, Ember?"

I shook my head. "No, but I do know how to swim. They taught us at the school I went to." We'd had a swimming pool and one of our P.E. modules had been swimming. I wasn't fast, but I enjoyed being in the water. Sometimes, I swam in the river behind my house, but it was usually too cold to enjoy.

"Well, that's one less thing for me to worry about you learning," Caleb teased.

I pinched his side, making him squirm away.

"Do you think it's okay for us to go considering the attack a few days ago?" Triston asked.

Caleb set his beer down and sighed. "Honestly, I would love to just hide Ember at my parents' place until we took the H.E. down, but it's not realistic. And I promised her that I'd show her the world, so starting with the beach seemed like a good idea. Hopefully, we won't run into any trouble while out, but Papa Dan is going to send a few werewolf guards with us and I think Papa Emrys is going to send Uncle Andras. Don't worry, they won't bother us, just be nearby in case we need their help."

It was sweet to see such a caring family.

"The guards will make me feel better," Triston said as he washed lettuce.

"I'll feel better, too," I admitted.

"Okay, good," Caleb said and exhaled softly.

Riddick and Branson showed up half an hour later, each carrying several bags of groceries.

I offered to help cook, but was denied, so I drank a beer and watched them. It was nice to see Branson smiling so much as he helped in the kitchen.

"You look happy," Riddick commented and sat on the chair beside me.

"I am happy," I said with a nod. "Thanks to you guys."

"It looks good on you," he said and squeezed my leg.

"Dinner is ready!" Branson announced. He and Triston carried the plates to the dining table while Caleb carried the salad and salad dressing.

Turning my chair around, I gasped at the chicken parmigiana. I hadn't been paying attention to what they were making, just watching them, so it was a pleasant surprise. "This looks delicious!"

"Let's eat!" Caleb said and handed me the salad bowl first.

"Thank you," I said and passed the salad to Riddick on my right. "For making the dinner and for everything you to do entertain me and make me happy."

"Thank you for existing and choosing us," Triston said.

"Yes, your existence is highly appreciated," Caleb said with a nod and stabbed some pasta.

"To Ember's existence!" Triston said and raised his beer.

Laughing and shaking my head, I raised my beer and so did the others.

"Ember's existence!" they all shouted.

CHAPTER
TWELVE

The drive to the beach was delayed by a trip to a store to buy me, Triston, and Branson bathing suits. Something we'd all not thought of until that morning.

By noon, we reached the beach and I was bouncing with excitement as we parked. There were some other people, but not as many as I'd thought there would be. To the left was also a boardwalk with games and restaurants.

"Swim, play on the beach, eat, and games in that order?" Riddick asked.

"Sounds good to me," I agreed.

"Last one in is a rotten egg!" Caleb shouted and ran towards the ocean as soon as his door was open.

Throwing open my door, I raced after him. I pulled off my coverup dress as I ran, but held it against my chest so I wouldn't lose it. I had just purchased it after all.

Caleb ran into the water until he was hip deep and then dove beneath the waves, moving until he was far enough out the waves didn't bother him. When he stood up out of the water, he flung his hair back, flinging water behind him and I staggered a step as I admired him and his now glistening abs.

Riddick ran past me, diving in beside Caleb.

Crap! I'd gotten distracted.

The first few steps of water were chilly and I yelped, but continued until I was hip deep, smiling when I realized it was warm water. I raised my arm up, keeping my coverup out of the water.

"Branson loses!" Caleb announced.

I turned and chuckled at the large man, toes barely touching the water.

"It's warmer in here!" I called out.

"I believe you," he said.

Caleb took my coverup and threw it to Branson. Turning, he grabbed me and dove with me under the water. Luckily, I'd anticipated what he had planned to do, so I'd taken a breath before we went under.

When we came up, I gasped in a breath and laughed.

"What type of sea life is common here?" Triston asked as he floated on his back beside us.

"If you're worried about sharks, they don't come this close to shore," Caleb said. "We do have jellyfish, but they are on the opposite side of the bay."

"I'm pretty sure a shark would flee if they sensed shapeshifters near them," I said and started floating, too.

Riddick and Caleb swam out into the deeper water, but even though I was pretty certain it would be fine, stayed where I was.

Triston floated beside me with his eyes closed. "What do you think of the ocean?" he asked.

"It's warmer than I thought it would be," I admitted. "The sound of the waves is definitely soothing, too."

"There are other oceans that are cold," he said. "Not nearly as much fun to swim in."

"Turtle!" Caleb called out.

I lowered my legs and looked towards the sound of his voice, and saw him pointing to my right. Turning, I saw the turtle swimming through the water. It was so big! Gasping, I swam closer, but then noticed a large fish swimming beside me and screeched.

Triston swam over, searching the water for danger, then chuckled. "It's just a fish. They won't bite you."

"It just startled me," I muttered, embarrassed.

"Come on, let's go build a sandcastle," he suggested.

I would have liked to swim a bit more, but I did also feel bad that Branson was on the beach by himself. He looked pretty comfortable, reclined on a lounge chair with an umbrella over him and sunglasses on. He also looked delicious as fuck with no shirt on, hands behind his head so his biceps were flexed and his lats out.

"Where did he get the chair and umbrella?" I asked.

"We brought them," Triston answered. "There's also body boards I think."

"What's that?"

"It's a small board that you can use in the water. Do you want to try that first?"

I nodded. "Yes. I would like to try it."

Triston raised his hand and Branson lowered his sunglasses. "Can you get a body board?"

Branson gave us a thumbs-up and headed back towards the SUVs.

"What are you guys doing?" Riddick asked as he and Caleb joined us.

"Branson's getting a body board for Ember to try," Triston answered.

"Oh! I didn't realize we had body boards," Caleb said. "After Ember plays with it, I'm going to try surfing on it."

"Surfing on it? It's too small," Riddick argued.

"You can surf in the shallows with it."

"I'll believe that when I see it," Triston said with a challenging smile.

"Oh, you'll see it," Caleb promised.

Branson returned with two body boards and threw them to us like a frisbee.

The board was light enough to float and had a rope with a wrap on it. "Secure that to you ankle or wrist," Triston explained. "Then come closer to shore so you can feel the waves going under you."

I did as he said and was smiling like a fool as I floated over the waves, up and down and up and down. "This is fun!" I shouted to them.

The three of them had moved to the shore to watch Caleb try to ride the body board.

I turned so I could face them and still ride the waves.

Caleb ran towards the water, threw the body board in front of him and tried to ride it across the water. He went barely a foot before falling and rolling in the waves.

Triston and Riddick laughed, but Caleb just grabbed the board and got up to try again.

He managed to do it for a bit on his tenth attempt and finally gave the board to Riddick for him to try.

Grabbing the board, I swam until I could touch the ground, then walked out of the water and handed the board to Triston. "That was fun."

He smiled. "I'm glad you enjoyed it."

"I'm going to build a sandcastle now," I said and walked over to Branson. "Want to help me build a sandcastle?"

He lowered his arms. "Sure."

We walked closer to the water, and started by digging the moat for the castle. Triston soon came over to help, building up a mound for the main part of the castle.

I tried to make a tower for the castle, but it just kept falling apart.

"You need to use sand that's a little wet," Branson explained. "That's the only way it'll stick together."

"Oh." I supposed that did make sense. If the dry sand stuck together, it would be weird to walk on.

"Building a sandcastle?" Caleb asked as he and Riddick joined us.

"Not very well," I muttered as I tried to dig down to get wet sand that would stick together.

"We'll help," Riddick said and dug his hands down into the water at the shoreline, and carried back the wet sand, placing it next to me.

I wasn't sure how long we sat there, silently working on our castle, but the sun was definitely lower when we finished and stood back to admire it.

It wasn't perfect, my spots were definitely crumbling, but it was done and castle-like.

Triston grabbed his phone from the lounge chair and snapped a picture. "Let's take a picture together," he suggested.

"Yes!" I agreed. We didn't have any pictures of all of us together. The only pictures I had found online were usually Caleb and I with the guys behind us, partially hidden. I wanted a picture I could save and print to put in my apartment.

The guys put me in the center and lined up around me.

Triston set his phone up, put a timer on the camera, then ran back to get in line beside Branson. "Smile!" he shouted.

I was already smiling, so it didn't matter.

Everyone's stomachs started growling, so we packed up our things, I put my coverup on, and we headed to the boardwalk to find some food.

It turned out there were only two restaurants, so Caleb flipped a coin to choose one. They nearly tripped over themselves to get us a table in any part of the restaurant we wanted. Caleb requested the second-floor balcony where we could see the ocean as we ate and a nearby table for our guards who I hadn't even noticed since we parked.

Skipping up the steps, I hummed a happy tune, trying to figure out what I was in the mood to eat.

The second floor was completely empty, which made it even nicer to be up there. Caleb and Branson took the seats at the patio rail, so I sat beside Caleb. Riddick sat at the head of the table and Triston sat beside Branson, across from me.

"This is the perfect afternoon spot," I said as I watched

the people playing on the beach and those walking by down below.

Triston nodded his agreement and opened his menu. "The weather is perfect today."

Our guards for the day, Andras, Martin, and Thor, sat at a table on the opposite side of the second floor, all turned so they could see the staircase, which was the only entrance to this area. I'd learned Martin was an ex-boyfriend of Jolie's and someone Caleb considered an uncle. He was really nice and hugged me when he introduced himself.

Opening my own menu, I looked over the available items and grew irritated at myself for being unable to make a choice. Everything sounded good and I couldn't decide.

"What's wrong, Ember?" Riddick asked.

"I want everything," I mumbled. "I can't decide."

Caleb folded his menu closed. "Perfect."

"Huh?" I asked, turning my head to look at him.

He just smiled and raised his hand for the waiter who was waiting nearby.

"How can I help you, Your Highness?" the waiter asked.

"We want one of everything on the menu, two pitchers of the house ale, and a cherry mimosa for the lady," Caleb ordered.

My eyes widened. Had he really just done that? Had he just ordered one of everything because I had said I wanted that?

"Right away, Your Highness," the waiter said and left to put in our orders.

"What?" Caleb asked when he saw my wide eyes. "I couldn't decide either, so this was the perfect solution."

My surprise turned into laughter.

"That's one way to find out if a restaurant is good or not," I said after I stopped laughing.

"Do you ever have to worry about poison?" Triston asked suddenly.

Caleb let out a bark of laughter. "Way to ask a dark question in a happy time, Tris."

Triston shrugged. "I just thought about it."

"No, I can smell the poisons. My dads spent a lot of time teaching me the various scents. So, when the food comes, I smell everything first, okay?"

"Aren't there poisons that don't have scents?" I asked. I swore I'd heard of some.

"No, that's only in the movies. Trust me, I can smell the sourness of a poison."

He seemed confident, but now I was worried. Was this why we ate at home so much? And why Jolie and her mates cooked without worrying about hiring a chef? Now that he mentioned it, I did remember him smelling my drink at the club before I took my first drink. Had that been why?

Caleb set his hand on my leg, which I hadn't realized I had started bouncing. "I promise. It'll be okay. Just let me smell the food first, yeah?"

"Okay," I breathed and leaned over to rest my head on his shoulder.

He tensed a second and then relaxed and stroked his thumb up and down the outside of my thigh where his hand sat.

The waiter returned with the beer pitchers and my drink. Caleb sniffed my drink, set it in front of me, sniffed the beer pitchers, and then nodded. The guys poured their drinks and we held the glasses up to tap them against each other to cheers.

"Today was great," I told them.

"The fun's not over yet!" Caleb exclaimed.

"Yeah, we've got games to play," Triston reminded me.

"Prizes to win," Caleb said.

"Prizes?" I asked. "What do you mean?"

Caleb laughed softly. "Didn't you watch movies and TV?"

"A bit, but honestly not very much. There was a lot of negativity and nasty things."

"What types of movies were you watching?" Riddick asked with a frown.

"Most of the games earn you a prize if you do it right," Caleb explained.

"Oh," I said. "Like what?"

"Stuffed animals mostly," he replied.

I had only had one stuffed animal, a bear that my parents had bought when I was very young, before my magic manifested. The school they shipped me to wouldn't allow me to bring it, so they'd thrown it away.

"Whoever wins the biggest or best prize gets Ember tonight," Caleb challenged.

"Oh, you're on," Branson said with a smirk. "I'm fantastic at carnival games."

"I like the confidence, bro. We'll see if you can back it up," Caleb replied.

Our food came out and we all waited tensely as Caleb smelled the food. He nodded and I bounced in my seat as I tried to decide what to eat first.

Caleb chose for me, grabbing the nearest dish, a double bacon cheeseburger, and cut it into fifths before giving me one of the pieces. He also divided up the fries and gave me my portion as well.

The others followed suit, dividing everything up into fifths so we could share them equally.

The fries were a bit soggy for my taste, so I divided my portion amongst the others on the plate, allowing them to have more fries.

By the time the plates were empty, my stomach felt like it might explode. Then my eyes landed on the chocolate cake the waiter brought out and I knew I was going to eat that as well.

Once our bill was paid, we headed out to play the games.

The games were definitely tricky and I quickly realized I was not going to win anything. The first game I tried was to toss a ball into a basket, a simple enough task, but the ball kept bouncing out.

Branson got three balls into his basket easily and won a large stuffed bear that reminded me of his animal form.

The next game as a shooting game and my aim was terrible! Triston destroyed us all, winning a picture of a tiger.

We approached the third game and I watched others playing it before I tried. The goal was to toss a plastic ring and get it to land around the neck of a glass bottle. None of us managed to do it, so we moved on to the next game.

This one was easier, you just had to toss a coin into one of the many glasses around the center of the stand and if your coin landed, you won that glass.

There was a short glass with a slightly rounded bottom

that would never spill as it just rolled in a circle. I took the three coins from the attendant and focused, ignoring all the sounds around us, and tossed.

My second coin landed inside the glass, spun around, and stayed inside! "Yes!" I shouted. "I got one!"

The attendant grabbed a box from beneath the booth and held it out to me. "Congratulations, Miss! Well done."

I hugged the glass against my chest, proud of myself. All five of us ended up with glasses and we bought a bag from a vendor with the name of the beach we were at to put the items we'd won inside as we continued down to play more games.

Three hours later, the bag was heavy from the items we'd all won and we had finally played all of the games.

"Are you ready to head home?" Caleb asked. "Or do you want to eat first?"

"I think I'd like to go home and eat together, if that's okay?" I said, swinging my arms in an exaggerated manner in my happiness.

"Sounds great to me," Triston said. "We can finish that board game we started last night."

"Yes," I agreed. "I need to know who the winner is."

Flagging down our guards, we went to the SUVs and climbed in, starting the long drive home.

"Did you have fun?" Martin asked.

I nodded vigorously. "So much fun! Those games and the food and the body board were all great."

"That makes me happy to hear," he said. "I took the liberty of snapping some pictures and will send them to

Caleb. I figured you might like to have them. I know my wife loves the candid pictures of us doing family things."

"Thank you!" That really was a super nice thing to do.

"I hadn't even thought about asking you guys to do something like that. Thanks, Uncle Martin," Caleb said.

Martin winked in the rearview mirror. "I've been married long enough to figure out a few things women like." He chuckled and looked back at the road.

"What do you want for dinner?" Branson asked me.

"Tacos," I said immediately. "With avocado and tomatoes and—"

Triston laughed. "We got it, darlin'. We'll make delicious tasting tacos that you will enjoy."

"And then I get to defeat you at our game!" I said confidently.

"Should we pull out all the prizes so you can decide the winner?" Caleb asked and opened the bag at his feet.

"Do we need a winner?" I asked. "Can we all stay together tonight?"

"We don't have a bed large enough for all of us," he reminded me.

"What about sleeping in the living room? We don't need to be in the same bed, just together." I wasn't sure why, but the urge to be with them all was immense.

"Okay," he said and set a hand on my leg. "We'll have a sleepover in the living room. I'll take the cushions off the coach and move the coffee table to give us enough room."

Leaning over, I kissed his cheek. "Thank you."

He rubbed his cheek against mine and whispered, "Anything for you, my queen."

CHAPTER
THIRTEEN

I woke with a start as the building shook.

"Earthquake?" Riddick asked, already on his feet.

We all lay in the living room on the couch cushions, our game last night going until two o'clock in the morning.

Glancing at the clock, I groaned when I realized we had only been asleep for four hours. "It's too early."

"That's not an earthquake," Caleb said and picked me up. "Come on, sleeping beauty, we need to figure out what's going on."

"What?" I asked and blinked the sleep out of my eyes.

"I think someone just bombed our building," he told me. "Or shot it with magic."

Instead of heading down towards the entrance, we went up to the roof.

My little garden of herbs was growing nicely despite the cold air.

I shivered in Caleb's arms as he handed me to Branson.

"I'm going to shift into my dragon form and fly up to see what I can find."

"You can put me down," I said and kissed his cheek. "I just wasn't fully awake yet."

Branson set me down, but immediately wrapped his arm around me and held me against his side to shield me from the wind and provide me warmth.

Caleb flew up into the air in his dragon form and circled the roof.

He truly was a gorgeous dragon.

Dropping back down to us, shifting to human form as he fell, he said, "There's a group of people along the street shooting magic at the building. We need to evacuate in case they cause it to fall."

"Fall?" I gasped. All of our belongings were in here.

"There are guards already headed towards them, but better safe than sorry," he explained. "Triston, you carry Branson and Ember, and I'll carry Riddick. Riddick and I will head down to help protect the building. You two go to the park across the street and wait there."

He was always separating our group and I hated it.

Leaning down, he brushed his lips over mine and said, "If anything happens, you run away, you hear me?"

"Not going to happen," I said and scoffed.

He growled. "Right, fine, just stay safe. Okay?"

I nodded. "You, too.

Riddick kissed my cheek then jumped up to grab Caleb's now dragon foot.

"I'm going to pick you up in each claw," Triston informed us. "That way I can fly more balanced."

I nodded my understanding and waited as he shifted and flew up into the air. He picked me up gingerly, keeping his talons away from my skin, and then picked up Branson. Quickly, he flew around the other side of the building, out of the range of the attacker's magic, and landed in the park.

They stood on either side of me, tense and ready for an attack.

My eyes were focused on Riddick and Caleb, battling the six mages who had been attacking our building with the help of three guards.

One of the mages used a spell that dropped Riddick to his knees.

I started to move forward, but Branson was already shifting into warrior form and running to help him.

Triston gripped my hand and pulled me in front of him. "Stay with me, Ember."

"I'm here," I said with a nod and squeezed our still joined hands.

Thankfully, they defeated the rest of the mages quickly and we were able to join the others. Triston kept his hold on my hand as we met up with them.

"Why does it seem like it's more often mages than others that attack us?" I asked softly.

"There were shifters attacking Ambrose and you, remember?" Triston replied.

"Yeah, right. Maybe I'm just still holding grudges against mages for my childhood." Though, I didn't have any issues with Nico.

"Everyone okay?" Triston asked Riddick and Branson. Caleb was nearby, but on his cell phone.

They nodded.

Riddick kicked one of the now dead mages. "He hit me with an electrocution spell."

"Those spells sting," I said and cringed, remembering when I'd been hit by one.

Caleb finished his call and said, "We're going to go to my parents' house for today. They want to have the apartment building inspected before we go back inside. Martin is on his way to pick us up now."

Looking around, I felt the hair on my nape on end. "We're really exposed out here," I whispered. "I feel like we're being watched too."

Branson rubbed the back of his neck and nodded. "Was just going to say that."

"Can you tell from where?" Caleb asked me.

Letting go of Triston's hand, I closed my eyes and turned in a slow circle, stopping when I felt that prickling sensation again. "Directly behind me," I whispered and opened my eyes.

"Let's move," Caleb said and headed down the sidewalk towards a little café we got breakfast from sometimes. "We'll be less exposed inside the café and I'll update Martin as to our location."

We started walking and I realized they'd put me in the center with each of them around me, Caleb in the front, Branson in the back, and Riddick and Triston on either side. Was this something they'd discussed and planned? Something they were making a habit?

"Ouch," I hissed as I stepped on a sharp rock on the sidewalk and hopped on one foot.

Caleb turned around, scooped me up into his arms, and resumed walking. It was so fast and smooth I didn't even get to gasp before he'd started walking again.

"Uh, thanks," I mumbled, embarrassed that I was the only one of the four of us that were barefoot to step on a rock.

"Triston and I put our dragon's scales on the bottom of our feet and Riddick and Branson shifted their feet into their animal form's," Caleb explained. "It's something you learn when you're little, so I didn't think about teaching it to you."

"So, shift my feet into my rabbit feet?" I asked.

He nodded. "They're tougher than your human skin so the rock wouldn't hurt as much."

Looking around his shoulder I saw he was right, the others had shifted their bare human feet into their animal's paws.

Riddick stepped forward and pushed open the café door, holding it so we could walk inside.

The café owner, Misty, a sweet older woman with bushy grey hair frowned at us. "Is everything alright, Your Highness?"

"I apologize for our appearance, Misty, but would you allow us to sit at a table while we wait for our driver?" Caleb asked and set me down on my feet.

"Of course, please, sit. Would you like something to eat or drink?" she asked and wiped off her hands on a towel.

"No, our ride should be here momentarily. Our wallets are also indisposed right now. Thank you for your hospitality."

She tsked, filled five to-go cup containers with water, put five cinnamon rolls in a box, and walked them over. "Nonsense. I know you're good for the money and even if you weren't, I can tell when someone is in need."

He bowed his head. "Thank you, Misty."

She patted his head and smiled. "Anything for my favorite customers." Looking down at me, she frowned. "Ember, your hair is a mess."

Reaching up, I felt it sticking up in different directions. "Sorry, we were woken up and had to evacuate our building so I didn't get to brush it or anything." I slapped a hand over my mouth, realizing I hadn't brushed my teeth yet either. "Oh, man. My breath is probably gross, too. Sorry!"

The guys chuckled and shook their heads.

"All of us have morning breath right now, Em. Don't worry about it," Riddick said.

"I think hers is the worst," Caleb said and took a bite of his cinnamon roll.

Misty hissed. "You be nice to your lady!"

He smiled. "Sorry."

She shook her head and looked at me. "You keep these men in line, you hear me? Don't let them walk all over you just because they're attractive. You deserve to be treated with respect, no matter if you're royal lineage or not. Every woman deserves to be treated like a queen and should treat her men like kings equally. Relationships have to be equal to last. Understand?"

I nodded and patted her hand. "Thank you, Misty."

A black SUV pulled up and we all stood, assuming it was Martin.

Four men in black outfits exited, raised staffs, which immediately started glowing.

134

Grabbing Misty, I looked at the sidewalk across the street, gathered my magic, and teleported all of us.

Misty gasped and gripped me tight. "Ember! You teleported."

"When did you learn that?" Riddick asked.

"Uh, I've been practicing it for about a month now," I admitted.

"Where'd they go?" one of the men yelled from the other side of the SUV.

"We're going to lead them away, Misty. You stay over here until we're gone and then return to your café, to safety. Okay?" Caleb instructed her.

She scowled. "I ain't weak, child. Just old." Walking confidently across the street, she stood in front of her café door and said, "Get out of here or I'll be forced to protect my café."

"We don't want any trouble with you, ma'am," one of the men said.

Martin pulled up, blocking our view and we all climbed into the SUV.

A spell hit the SUV, but Martin floored before any other attacks could hit.

He looked in the rearview mirror as we headed towards the house. "You okay?"

"Yes," Caleb said. "Thanks for picking us up."

"Aw, we forgot the cinnamon rolls," I whined.

"There should be food at the house," Riddick said. "If not, we'll order stuff."

Martin opened the center console and pulled out a granola bar. "Here, as a father, I always keep a snack or two in the car."

"Yes!" I shouted and tore it open, shoving the entire thing in my mouth. Closing my eyes, I sighed happily as I ate it.

"Apparently teleportation magic makes her hungry," Branson said with a chuckle.

"Wait, what? She teleported?" Martin asked.

Caleb nodded. "Dad taught her the basics and apparently the sneaky minx has been practicing in secret."

Something hit the back of the SUV, making it swerve a bit, but Martin quickly got it back under control.

Looking behind us, we found the SUV that had pulled up to Misty's café following us, a mage out the top shooting spells at us.

I groaned, leaned over the seat, and said, "I'm so over this." Holding my hand out, I used my magic to grip the SUV's driver's side tire and crushed it. For added safety, I crushed the front passenger tire as well. Turning back around, I sat back in my seat and smiled. "There, now they can't follow us."

All eyes were on me.

Caleb bent and kissed me deeply, his tongue sweeping across mine and making my heart flutter. He pulled back so he could look at me, his eyes glowing. "That was so hot."

"I'm in the car," Martin reminded him. "Wait until you get to the house to maul each other."

"Spoilsport," Caleb teased, but as he shifted in his seat and put his arm around my shoulders, there was an obvious bulge in his sweatpants.

Averting my gaze, I hid my smile from him.

FOURTEEN

The guys offered to make breakfast, but I shooed them all out so I could cook the meal for a change. While I appreciated them making me food all the time, I wanted to be a contributing member to our pack as well.

Caleb tried to come in twice, but I kicked him out each time. He pouted, but obeyed, even stuck his bottom lip out the second time. I held strong despite it and didn't even laugh like I wanted to.

With so many shifters to feed, it required a lot of food. Thankfully, there were ingredients to make pancakes and a flat iron cooktop so I could cook several at once. I put two trays of bacon in the oven, cracked and scrambled two dozen eggs, made hashbrowns by shaping them into five rectangles on the flat iron cooktop, diced up and cooked spinach and bell peppers to mix into the scrambled eggs. I also added a bit of shredded cheese to the scrambled eggs, since I knew Branson liked cheese in his eggs.

Sweating, but smiling profusely as I finished putting all

the food on platters, I called out, "Food is ready!"

Caleb, Riddick, Branson, and Triston walked into the kitchen. Their eyes widened at the food, but they silently grabbed a platter of food each, and carried them to the dining table.

"Everything smells delicious," Branson praised me.

"Thanks," I said. "Hopefully, it tastes good, too."

Triston went back into the kitchen and came back with a mimosa in hand, making my eyes widen. He winked. "I thought you might enjoy a drink after saving us earlier and cooking us a feast."

I rolled my eyes. "I didn't save us and this is hardly a feast."

"You did save us. Those four mages were pretty powerful and it would have been a pain to fight them. You protected us," Riddick argued.

My cheeks burned and I said, "Well, you and Caleb protected us earlier. That's what pack does, right? We protect each other?"

Caleb scowled and didn't reply, but the others nodded.

"Let's eat before it gets cold!" I said, changing the subject since it clearly bothered him.

Branson and Riddick made my plate for me and instead of getting upset, I sat back and let them, remembering Leona's. It was nice to feel so appreciated and valued.

After he finished eating his food, Caleb excused himself and disappeared.

Branson, Riddick, and Triston went to the kitchen to clean up and said they were headed to the game room to play after, but I wasn't in the gaming mood yet.

Closing my eyes, I pictured Caleb, felt within me for the connection we had, and followed it as I walked through the house. Occasionally, I cracked an eye open just to make sure I wasn't about to walk down some stairs or into a door, but after a few minutes, I found him in his bedroom staring out the window at the woods. Standing just inside the doorway, I waited, knowing he sensed I was there.

He took a shuddering breath before finally speaking, still facing the window. "As soon as I could talk, Papa Dan started treating me like a fellow alpha, a king. He tried to teach me everything he could about how to be a good leader. Being an alpha is one thing, but being a king requires a lot more."

Sitting down on the edge of his bed, I stayed silent, letting him say what he needed to.

"Mom was against it at first, thinking it was too much to teach a child, but Papa Emrys and Papa Katar also agreed. So, they began doing the same. Each race has different challenges, many similar challenges of course, but there are some unique ones as well. When I met Riddick, I realized that there was a reason they'd been teaching me that. Someday, I will become the King of the Hybrids. You could argue that I already am, but I won't accept that title until we have a place for our people and our pack grows. Now ... now I'm wondering if I will ever be ready to accept that title. How can I offer protection to others when I'm constantly fighting for my own safety? When my little pack of five is attacked daily?"

His shoulders hunched forward and he shook his head.

Standing, I walked up behind him and set my hand on the center of his back. "A king isn't always ready when he becomes one. Nico wasn't prepared, but he accepted the role and he's been working to improve himself every single day. Silverowl told me about some of the trials and things Nico dealt with. Dan has failed a time or two. I bet all of them have, if you ask them. What makes a good king isn't one who is perfect, but one who is constantly willing to put his people before himself."

He spun around and stared down at me. "Which is also what I lack. When I saw you in danger in the park, saw those men after you, I stopped worrying about Ambrose, my only thought was you."

Smiling up at him, I shrugged a single shoulder. "Isn't that common, too? For you to put the person you have feelings for before others?"

He canted his head a bit, reminding me of his wolf, and asked, "Are you saying you have feelings for me, Ember?"

"I think that's pretty obvious, Caleb."

He cupped my cheek and said, "I can't stand the thought of you being hurt. If you were to be seriously injured or ..." He shook his head, unwilling to say it. "... it will crush me."

I placed my hand over his and said, "Then let's fight side by side, protecting each other's backs. No more splitting us up. No more sending me to a safe spot with one or two of our pack. We fight together as one unit. All five of us."

He sighed and dropped his head down until his forehead rested against mine. Drawing in a few, silent breaths, he finally whispered, "Okay."

"See, another sign of a good king. One who listens."

Chuckling, he stepped back and poked at my side. "Is

that so? One who listens? Are you saying that you're always, right?"

"If the shoe fits," I said and swatted his hand away while backing up to keep him from tickling me again.

He darted forward, his fingers tickling my side again, causing me to squeak and laugh. "I didn't know bunnies wore shoes," he teased.

Running away from him, I jumped down the stairs and headed towards the game room.

Yelling over my shoulder, a smile as wide as any I could make, I said, "Don't you know, rabbits have lucky feet!"

We ended up staying at Caleb's parents' house until they returned due to our apartment needing some minor repairs. Thankfully, it wasn't anything that couldn't be fixed in a few days.

When the SUV pulled up the day of his parents' return, we all waited outside the house, knowing it was bound to be a rambunctious reunion.

As expected, when Caleb's dads got out of the vehicle, they immediately headed for him, pouncing on him in the grass as well as Riddick and to their surprise, Branson and Triston.

Jolie pulled me into a bone crunching hug. "Oh, Ember! Are you okay? You poor thing. I think I may have cursed you with my danger attraction."

I returned her hug, trying not to cry at the emotions swirling within me as she voiced her honest concern for my safety and hugged me like I'd always wished my mother would have. "I'm okay," I reassured her. "They kept me safe and with the ability to hide in your house, we were good."

She pushed me back and frowned down at me. "You've changed."

My brows rose. "What?"

Her frown turned into a smile. "In a good way. You're finally accepting that you are part of their pack and that you aren't a stinky little hermit anymore."

"Hey!" I said, but laughed knowing I did on occasion smell pretty awful when I was up for several days in a row tending to an injured patient.

"They're going to be fighting for a bit, come inside and tell me everything that's happened, especially about your sleepover at Leona's," she said, linked her arm through mine, and pulled me into the house.

Glancing over my shoulder, I caught Caleb's eye just long enough to get a wink from him.

Once inside, Jolie spun around and set her hands on my arms, whispering so quiet it was hard to hear her, "I heard you used a teleportation spell."

I nodded.

"Good. You're in more danger than you or Caleb realize. We did some investigating while we were on vacation and the roots of H.E. have spread even farther than we dared think. I am going to teach you a spell, one you must only use in the deadliest situation, one where you think all hope is lost."

My eyes widened and my heart pounded as she stared into my eyes, relaying information that was terrifying.

"This spell, if done correctly and if your power is enough, will ensure that you can all get to safety. A friend of mine has premonitions and she urged me to teach you. I dare not ignore her."

"What is the spell?" I asked.

"A portal spell," she answered. "You can create a portal door to a place that you've been before. This spell is one you can create and open beneath the feet of yourself and your pack, to send them to a safe location. Like this house! It requires a lot of magic for a single portal, so we're going to spend the next two weeks devoting every hour of your training to learning to make portals, to teleport not just yourself, but all five of you." She paused and cupped my cheeks. "You cannot tell your pack about this, especially not Caleb. As future king, he will not want an escape plan like this, especially because the magic requires a lot from you." She paused. "It not only requires magic, but blood. Not a lot! But blood magic is heavily frowned upon despite it not being evil. Caleb especially sneers at it and this spell will be seen as a coward's way out. He will not want you to risk yourself to save him. I cannot see my son, my only child, die because he is stubborn like his fathers ... and his mother."

Setting my hands on hers, I smiled and said, "I understand. Any training I can get is worth it."

She pressed a soft kiss to my forehead and said, "Good. Now, let's go to Nico's lab and start your first day of training."

FIFTEEN

Jolie wasn't joking when she said the training would be grueling. Every single night I crawled into my bed, exhausted and depleted of magic, energy, and mental focus.

Caleb was growing more and more concerned, probing his mother and I for information, but we managed to avoid answering directly about our training.

Each night, one or more of the guys would slip into my room and sleep with me, but my wearied state meant no time for sexy shenanigans. The mornings were a different story.

After one such morning, I lay cuddled between Triston and Riddick, sweat slicked and panting.

"Can I ask you both something?" I whispered, feeling my nerves building at what their answers might be.

"Of course," Triston said and traced my jaw with his pointer finger.

"Why haven't either of you marked me?"

Both tensed and held their breaths.

It was a solid forty-five seconds before either moved.

"We're worried about possibly creating a mating bond with you if more of us mark you, you know that," Triston replied with a small smile, one that didn't reach his eyes.

"With two of us having a mark on you, it already keeps other males away and provides our pack's scent to let them know you are in ours," Riddick added.

Frowning, I rolled over and asked, "So, you don't want to mark me?"

His eyes dropped to my shoulder where my mark from Branson was visible. "We definitely want to mark you, but we don't want to take away your option to choose."

"What if ... I want to be marked by you both? What if I think the risk is worth it?"

Both tensed again, Riddick, who I faced was the first to ask.

"Are you saying you want to be mated to us, Ember? This is a very serious discussion, not one to take lightly."

"And it is not something to be discussed just between the three of us, but the entire pack," Triston added softly behind me.

Closing my eyes, feeling foolish, I nodded. "Right, yes, of course." I didn't know for certain that all four of them *wanted* to be fully mated to me. The courting time wasn't just for the females, but the males as well. Everyone had to make their decision as to whether they wanted to be mated or not.

For all I knew, Riddick didn't want to be mated, but only wanted to keep the connection we had until he was absolutely certain. It had only been a couple months, after all. I was moving too quickly.

Climbing out of the bed, I hurried to the bathroom, brushing my teeth to try to distract my brain and stop the tears stinging at the back of my eyelids.

Riddick knocked on the bathroom door. "Ember? Are you okay?"

I needed a break. I needed to breathe somewhere alone, somewhere I could truly be alone. "I need some time alone," I told him.

"Okay," he said softly. "We'll head downstairs to help with breakfast."

No, he didn't understand. I couldn't be *here* right now. There were nine people in this house, maybe more of there were guards or Leona and her men. I needed pure quiet.

Closing my eyes, I pictured my cabin, or the smoldering wreckage that was left, envisioning a rectangle opening just about roof height, gathered my magic, and opened a portal beneath my feet.

I fell with a yelp, but my feet quickly hit the dirt, and I opened my eyes to find myself in the dirt yard in front of what used to be my cabin.

With a small smile, that was short-lived, I gave myself a mental pat on the back for successfully using a portal and landing without falling like I had several times this week in my training.

Yes, I could have teleported instead, but I wanted to ensure my portals were as perfect as my teleporting.

Immediately, I felt a tug on the center of my chest, one that felt like Caleb, but I couldn't be sure.

Shaking out my hands, I walked over to my hammock between two large trees on the inside of my border, lay down and closed my eyes as it rocked back and forth.

Drawing in a deep breath, I fully relaxed as I enjoyed the peace of being away from others. The sounds of the forest, birds calling, animals rustling through the underbrush, the river, combined to create a lullaby to ease my anxiety and fears.

What would it mean if one or more of them didn't want to mate with me? Should I just wait longer, to see how our relationship continues to progress? It was too soon, wasn't it? This was my first time in a relationship, perhaps I was still in my lust phase.

No. Shaking my head, I knew that wasn't the case. I loved them. Even if it felt insane to admit that.

Slowly, the panic ebbed away and I was able to relax. To accept that I needed to give them all more time to decide what they wanted to do. I wouldn't bring up the marks again or mating until they were all ready to discuss it.

After several hours of relaxing, I felt the tugging on my chest from not just one, but four parts.

Was it the guys trying to get my attention? Maybe something was wrong.

Climbing out of my hammock, I gathered my magic, and this time used a portal to return to my bathroom.

Opening my eyes, I found my bathroom door torn off the hinges and thrown onto my bed. "Uh, did I do that?" I whispered in horror. Had I blown the door of when I used the portal? That hadn't happened in any of my practices!

"Ember!" Caleb yelled, his voice deeper than normal as

he ran into the room. His eyes were wide, frantic, and he was in a warrior form. He raced to me, grabbed my arms, and spun me around. "Are you okay? What happened? Where did you go?"

Riddick, Branson, and Triston ran inside my room behind him, their chests heaving.

"I'm fine, I just needed some space," I told him.

He froze, looked down into my eyes and asked, "You teleported away?"

I nodded. "I went to my property for a bit. I was feeling really anxious, like a panic attack was about to happen, and just needed to be alone."

He dropped his hands and took a step back. "You could have come to us."

My brows furrowed. "I needed to be alone, Caleb."

He shifted into his fully human form and backed up another step. "You needed to be away from us."

Technically, yes, but ...

"Why are you so upset?" I asked softly.

"We thought you'd been kidnapped or something," Branson explained. "You disappeared and it felt like you were really far away."

"Nico couldn't trace your teleportation, though," Riddick said, scowling. "Did you block it or something?"

Of course he couldn't trace my teleportation, since I had used a portal instead.

"I'm sorry to have worried you all," I said. "Next time I'll make sure to say something."

Caleb turned and left the room without another word.

"Are you okay now?" Triston asked and took a step

forward, his hand out, but quickly dropped it and stepped back.

Why were they acting like this?

"Yes, I'm fine. Like I said, I just needed to be alone for a bit to collect my thoughts. The sounds of the forest help me calm down and relax." And to come to a decision about giving them time and space to decide on their own how they wanted to move forward. Changing quickly, I turned and said, "I'm starving. I'm going to get some food."

They stepped to the side, letting me pass, and for the first time no one offered to make me food.

Scowling, I looked at their faces and realized they all looked sad.

"What's wrong?" I asked.

Branson turned and left, slamming his door behind him as he went into his room.

"Nothing, go on and get some food," Triston said and smiled weakly before heading to his own room.

I looked at Riddick, but he clenched his jaw, turned away, and headed to his room as well.

"Why are they so upset?" I whispered. Was it because I had worried them needlessly? I apologized, though.

Uncertainty spread within me and I gnawed on my lower lip. Should I go talk to them? I didn't want to explain what I'd been thinking about, that would negate my decision.

My stomach grumbled and clenched in pain. Decision made, food first.

As I made a sandwich, Jolie walked in and stared at me. "What happened?"

"Uh, I used a portal successfully."

She frowned. "Why were the guys freaking out earlier? It sounded like Caleb broke something and they dragged Nico upstairs to your room looking frantic."

"I needed some space, so I went to my cabin to think for a bit. They thought I'd been kidnapped." I flinched. "I should have told them I was leaving."

Her eyes widened. "Ember, there is an organization bent on killing you and you left your pack, teleporting hundreds of miles away? Of course they were upset! I'm upset now!"

Setting down the butter knife, I frowned. "I'm an adult, a woman who needs the occasional solitary moment. Are you saying I can't have that?"

"You aren't a solitary woman anymore. You are part of a pack, a pack that cares deeply about you. If you need to be alone, you tell them and go out in the forest behind the house. What if they had someone watching your place? What if they'd attacked you while you were alone? You could have been killed or captured and executed!"

My initial urge was to yell at her, but after taking a breath and thinking about what she said, I realized she was right.

I was an asshole.

"I'm sorry," I whispered.

"I'm not the one you should be apologizing to, Ember." She set her hands on my shoulders and said, "I know it's hard. I know this life is much different from the one you've been living for twenty years. But it's not just your life anymore. If you get kidnapped, or killed, Caleb will go on a rampage. He will leave behind a bloody warpath that will change him and possibly the world. You have a responsibility to not just yourself now, but those men as well."

Nodding, I grabbed my sandwich and headed towards the stairs, head hanging in shame.

It was time to put on my big girl panties and apologize to them.

Standing in the hallway, I stared at the doors and debated who I should apologize to first. I had known Branson the longest, but Caleb was our alpha.

Taking a big bite of my sandwich, I waited just long enough to eat it before heading to Caleb's door. Knocking twice, I waited, but he didn't respond. Slowly, I pushed it open and peeked inside.

Caleb was on the floor, shirtless, doing pushups with his headphones on. After ogling him for a minute, I walked in, purposefully making my footsteps harder, and sat on his bed.

He turned his head, looked at me, then did one more pushup before sitting back on his heels and taking his head-phones off. "You made a sandwich?"

I nodded. "And came here to apologize."

He looked down at his hands dangling between his bent legs.

"If it's alright with you, I would like to set up a hammock in the woods here, so I can go there if I need to gather my thoughts in the future."

His head raised and he said, "You're welcome to build whatever you want, including a cabin if you would like it."

I smiled softly and said, "I don't need a cabin on your parent's land, but I appreciate the offer. I'll wait until I have my own land, or my pack buys land, and build one there."

He stood and walked to me, towering over me for a

breath before dropping to his knees and cupping my face. "You scared me, Ember."

I set my hand on his face and he leaned into it. "I'm sorry for scaring you."

He sat on the bed beside me and set his hand behind me. "What set you off this morning? Is it something I can help you with? Do you want to talk about it?"

"No," I said and shook my head. "I'm okay now."

"Tomorrow, we'll go back to the apartment, okay?"

I nodded, kissed his cheek, and stood. "I'm going to talk to the others." Turning towards the door, I found the rest of them there. Bowing my head, I said, "I'm sorry for worrying you all and disappearing without saying anything. I promise not to do that in the future. I'm not used to having people care about me or my location."

"Are you sure you don't want to talk about this morning?" Triston asked.

"Yes, I'm fine now."

He and Riddick scowled, but didn't say more.

"Are we good?" I asked, looking around at all four of them.

They nodded.

Smiling wide, I clapped my hands together. "Great! Now, let's go downstairs so I can destroy you all at karting!"

"Did you just challenge the reigning champion?" Caleb asked and stepped around me.

"You are about to lose that title," I said confidently and headed out of the room.

"Challenge accepted," Caleb said from behind me.

CHAPTER
SIXTEEN

"I don't like this," Caleb said, and growled as he paced back and forth across the living room.

We'd just learned that there was going to be a meeting of the higher-ups in the Hybrid Eradication Organization, or H.E. and it was in the city near us with a great opportunity for someone to sneak close and eavesdrop.

"You're too powerful to sneak in somewhere to try to spy on others," I reminded him. "We can feel you coming a mile away." I sat on the couch, watching him pace, and trying my best to keep calm and relaxed to try to ease his tension. So far, it hadn't worked.

Triston lounged on the end of the couch, looking bored. "Caleb, everyone knows what you look like, especially those that are part of the H.E."

"They seem to be after Ember as well, remember? So, they know what she looks like, too," Caleb countered. His eyes darted to me before he resumed looking at the floor as he paced across it.

"Not in my rabbit form," I said. "Only a few of the members of the H.E. have seen me in it, and they're all dead. I have enhanced hearing in my rabbit form, I've improved it a lot thanks to Silverowl's training, so I should be able to hear them easier than any of you. Plus, I can sense wards if there are any, so I won't trip them, and now that I can teleport, I'm the best one of us to send to spy. I'll be the safest one."

He growled and continued pacing, hands clenched into fists at his sides.

"I don't like it either, but she is the best option," Riddick said from the corner of the living room he stood in. It was like he was trying to blend into the darkness in the corner while he brooded.

Branson had been silent, scowling, and sat in one of the reclining chairs staring at the muted television showing the news.

"I can alert you guys if I do get in trouble," I said. "If there's an issue, I can just tug on our connection and you'll know immediately that I need help. You can be stationed nearby ready to come in should I need extraction."

Caleb's nostrils flared and he turned to look at me. "Prove it."

"Prove what?" I asked.

"Tug on them. Prove you can do it."

It had become easier and easier to feel them, the bonds within my chest that connected me to each of the four men in the room. Caleb's was the brightest and strongest of the connections, glowing in a way the other's didn't. I gave it a sharp tug twice and saw him stumble a step forward, his eyes growing wide. I did the same to all of them to make sure they could all feel it.

Branson grunted when I did it to him, but didn't shift his eyes from the television.

"See? I can do it easily now."

Caleb dropped to his knees in front of me, his hands rested on my thighs, and he stared straight into my eyes. His bright blue eyes glowed as he gripped my legs. "The instant you are in trouble, you alert us, you understand? You are more important than spying on them, so if you can't get past security or wards safely, you can just come back. We won't be disappointed or anything. Okay?"

I cupped his face with my hands and pressed a light kiss to his lips. "I will be safe and not put myself in any situation that might be unnecessarily risky. I promise."

Ever since my trip to my lands, he'd been exceptionally protective. He'd even growled at Fox when he'd thrown me over his shoulder during a sparring match. Thankfully, Fox had just laughed at the situation.

Caleb stood and headed towards the stairs. "The meeting is supposed to happen in two hours."

Branson followed him out, leaving me with Riddick and Triston.

Triston lifted his arm, inviting me to come lay against his side.

I accepted, tucking myself against him and resting my head on his chest. "Thank you."

Riddick sat down on my other side and unmuted the television, scowling heavily.

Reaching over, I set my hand on his where it sat on the

couch. After a brief hesitation, he turned his hand over and laced our fingers together.

Triston rested his head atop mine.

We sat like that until it was time for us to go.

The drive to the coffee shop where the guys would wait was silent and tense and my siren abilities were not helping at all, so I stopped trying to relax them.

Ezio sat at a different table than us, in the corner where he could see the entire shop and the doors to the back and the entrance. As soon as we walked in, the people inside began whispering and a few took pictures.

Caleb, Riddick, and Branson sat with scowls while Triston and I chatted, smiled, and laughed.

When it was time for me to leave, I hugged each of them, saving Caleb for last. As my arms wrapped around his shoulders, he pulled me down onto his lap, slid his hand around the back of my head, and kissed me deeply.

Someone gasped and I saw a few flashes of light from people taking pictures, but didn't care.

When he finally pulled back, he traced a finger over my swollen lower lip and said, "I'll be there as soon as you call."

Giving him a warm smile, I said, "I know." Pressing one more kiss to his lips, I stood and walked to the back where the restrooms were and the back door I was using to leave. The meeting was taking place in a warehouse district four blocks away. Since it was mainly used for storage, there wouldn't be very many people walking about, which meant I would need to get close, then shift into my rabbit form and slowly hop my way through the yards to the right warehouse.

The entire trip took me thirty minutes due to how slow I was in rabbit form, but I made it to the warehouse finally. Hiding beneath a rusted truck, I watched the people on watch walking around the perimeter and surveyed the layout. There were four of them, spread out and moving in a continual circle. Along the side of the warehouse was a variety of items like wooden pallets, large metal trash cans, and broken machines and parts. There were windows along the side of the building I could see and a door on the front where a few people had gone inside a couple of minutes ago. To the right of the warehouse was a large building with roll up doors that appeared to be a vehicle repair or storage place. The guards weren't going down the alleyway between the buildings, but I wasn't sure where the meeting would take place to know if I could use the alleyway.

Timing it just right, I waited for one guard to walk by my hiding spot, then hopped as fast as I could, galloping until I reached the closest side of the building, and hid between the building and a wooden pallet leaned against it. My heart hammered from the run, but after staying perfectly still long enough to see the next guard pass by, it slowed as I confirmed I had made it without detection.

Step one, infiltrate the perimeter, complete.

Making my ears bigger, I focused my power on my ears to increase their hearing. The window I sat under had no voices, but I could hear some deeper in the building. Hopping around the side of the building, hugging the edge, I followed the voices down the alleyway to the opposite corner from where I started. The voices converged in that corner, at least a dozen of them from what I could tell.

In front of me was a large metal dumpster with the two lids closed, to the right of it a broken ladder rested against it. Due to the location, being in the alleyway, the perimeter guards wouldn't look down this way on their rounds, so I should be able to peek into the window for at least a second to confirm this was the meeting room.

Hopping onto the first step of the ladder, I froze as it wobbled. When it didn't fall over or make a noise that would alert the guards, I exhaled a shaky breath and hopped up to the next step, continuing until I hopped onto the lid of the trash bin. The window was covered by newspapers, making it hard to see inside, but there was a corner torn by the edge. Being careful, I peered inside.

Confirmed, there were over a dozen people inside, and sitting at the front of the room were my adoptive parents. They sat with angry scowls on their faces while the people milled about and talked.

Looking around the room more, I noticed there were pictures on one of the walls. Pictures of Caleb, Riddick, Branson, Triston, me, and several other people I didn't recognize. Were they other hybrids? Ones they were going to go after?

My adoptive dad stood and people immediately stopped talking, heading to sit in chairs that were arranged facing him.

"Let's get this meeting started. We don't have much time and don't want to risk detection. The recent failures and captures of some of our members has increased the need for discretion," Dad said gruffly.

"What positive news do you have for us?" Mom asked.

A tall, thin woman with a scar on her chin walked up to

the wall of pictures, grabbed one, and tore it in half. "We killed this hybrid last night."

My chest tightened and with it came both sadness and fury.

"Has the investigation into the prince's weaknesses garnered anything?" Mom asked.

A man with long, silver hair that hung to his belt stood. "One thing is clear, he prioritizes the girl's safety over his own and others. She would be perfect bait to take him out."

"We've known that since we first saw them together," Mom scoffed.

"As a true hybrid, he doesn't have many weaknesses. Only emotional ones that we've found so far, but we do know that whenever he is training they are focusing on him fighting multiple opponents and he seems to struggle with that," the man added.

"So we need to overwhelm them with numbers, separate the girl from him, and then we'll be able to defeat him," Dad said and nodded.

"To pull off an attack of that scale, we'll need to call in our fringe members and to get the hybrid scum somewhere his family won't be able to show up quickly to jump in to help."

Mom waved the concern away. "We'll figure that out after this. What other news do you have?"

"We've located this hybrid," a short, petite woman said as she limped over to the pictures and pointed at one of the people I didn't know. "We're surveilling them now to determine the best time to attack them and should have an attack ready to go by next week at the latest."

"Wonderful," Dad said. "We look forward to hearing about your success."

Success in murdering someone. They were truly horrendous people.

"How is the weapon progressing?" Mom asked.

A large, man with a bushy beard covering his face stood and said, "We used it on the hybrid that we killed last week and it cut through their dragon scales like butter. It is ready to be used against the prince without issue. It will kill him even if he tries to use scales to protect himself."

A sword that could cut through dragon scales? That was impossible! How had they developed something like that?

"How are the magic preparations going on the mage side?" Dad asked.

"The implosion spell is harder to use than we anticipated. Only three are able to use it so far," a man off to the side answered. "We're working on an alternative magic, one that will be strong enough to damage their scales to allow for breaks in their defense that way."

These magic spells and weapons were not only dangerous for hybrids, but all of us. I needed to tell Jolie and her mates as well. This was terrifying.

They talked about a few other magic items, weapons, and spells that had me chilled to the bone.

When they finished their meeting, I hopped down and hid beneath the dumpster, scrunching my nose at the smell, but stayed still and silent five minutes after the last car drove by.

Hopping out slowly, I stayed along the wall, listening for any noises to indicate someone had stayed behind.

Hiding behind the wooden pallet I had first gone to, I waited another ten minutes to confirm no perimeter guards were left. Just as I was about to hop away, I heard a voice from the front of the building. Hopping closer, I peeked around and saw Dad talking to a mage.

"I don't care what you have to do. The next fight, you must kill Ember. Her death will weaken the prince and allow us the chance we need to take him out."

"You don't want to capture her and use her to make him surrender?" the mage asked.

"No, if there's a chance she can be saved, he won't give up. She must die. Cut her head off in front of him or stab her through the heart. Just make sure he sees her die."

Pain at this betrayal, this confirmation that he did not love me, had me stumbling back against the building, tears in my eyes making it hard to see. I knocked into the wooden pallet, causing it to fall with a loud bang.

"What was that?" Dad demanded.

Running as fast as I could, I headed into the fields of rusted vehicles where they wouldn't see me and kept running until I was sure I had lost them, my vision clouded by tears no matter how much I tried to get them to stop.

When I ran into the busier streets of the city, I had to dodge people's feet, making a few women in club dresses scream as I hopped between their legs and towards the coffee shop.

Caleb's eyes snapped up as he saw me through the window of the coffee shop and he ran outside, scooping me up into his arms. "What's wrong?" he asked. "Are you injured?"

"Get in the SUV," Ezio ordered us.

Caleb climbed in, still cradling me against his chest. He wiped at my tears, but they continued to flow.

Was I doomed to be betrayed by everyone who should have loved me? Would I end up hated by Caleb and my pack just like my parents and adoptive parents?

Was I truly unlovable?

SEVENTEEN

Ezio drove us to a high rise building in the center of downtown and took us up to a conference room where all of the kings, queens, princes, and princesses waited.

It had taken ten minutes for me to calm down enough to shift into my human form and even then, my chest hurt and tears felt imminent, but I held them at bay.

Once they had confirmed I wasn't injured, the guys set their hands on me, providing me silent comfort.

Looking out the window at the city below us, I waited and felt a numb feeling starting to spread within me.

"Okay, Ember, tell us what you learned," Caleb said.

"They're developing new weapons and magic spells," I started. "Ones that do damage previously thought impossible."

"Like what?" Nico asked.

I turned and said, "They have a sword that they claimed can easily cut through dragon scales."

Emrys and Rhys growled.

"A magically enhanced sword?" Nico asked.

I shrugged. "They didn't go into specifics about the sword, but ..." My throat tightened and I swallowed hard before continuing. "... they said they killed a hybrid and it cut through their scales like butter." Looking at Rhys I said, "They're planning to decapitate Caleb with it."

Everyone in the room growled and Jolie slammed her hands on the table as she stood and began to pace along one wall of the room.

"What else?" Katar asked softly.

I told them everything that I had learned and tried to describe some of the pictures on the walls. Riddick pulled up some pictures on his phone and I was able to confirm two of them. I left only one thing out, the conversation at the end by my dad and the mage. If I told Caleb, he wouldn't have let me continue going with them on missions and I wasn't going to let him go out and fight without me. If he went without me and got killed when I could have prevented it, I would never forgive myself.

They started talking amongst themselves, trying to figure out plans to find the ones who were creating the weapons and magic spells. I sat down against the wall next to the window and watched the people walking about looking like ants. They were moving about their lives none the wiser to the terrible things that were being plotted.

Ezio squatted down in front of me, drawing my attention from the city. "What aren't you telling them?" he asked softly.

"I've told them everything," I said and turned my gaze back to the window.

"You didn't come back crying because of what you told us. What did you hear, Ember? I can tell, you learned something you don't want them to know. What is it?"

"What are you two whispering about?" Caleb asked.

Ezio made some sign with his hand I didn't see and Caleb stayed where he was instead of walking closer.

"If what you know could end up protecting them or saving them, don't you think you should share it?" Ezio asked softly. "Don't you want them to know everything so they can better prepare themselves for the fight that is coming?"

He did have a point.

"I heard my adoptive dad ..." My throat tightened as my chest throbbed in pain and tears built again. Dammit, why was this causing me so much trouble when I had been separated from them for so long? Why was it increasing my fear of abandonment? "... he ordered a mage to murder me no matter what it took." I raised my eyes to his and the tears started falling. "He read me bedtime stories and played tea party with me. Now, he wants my head cut off. My birth parents gave me up and now my adoptive parents are going to have me murdered. What's next, me being banished to protect Caleb?"

Jolie dropped to her knees beside me and pulled me into a hug. "No. No, nothing is going to happen to you, Ember." She sniffled. "I already told you, even if you left Caleb and his pack right now, you would always be welcome with us. You aren't going to be abandoned."

Caleb pushed Ezio away from me. "Stop making her cry," he growled. Sitting down, he took my hands, while his mother held me, and stared into my eyes. "Talk to me."

Wiping the tears from my eyes, I exhaled harshly and gathered myself together. No more weeping. I had to move past these insecurities. Yes, I had a fear of abandonment among other issues, but it was time to work on improving that. Would it hurt if Jolie banished me to protect Caleb or for Caleb to send me away? Yes. But as my life was teaching me, I wasn't truly in charge and needed to learn to move forward as best as I could with what happened. My first step was being honest with Caleb, even if he tried to leave me behind. "I'm your weakness, Caleb. They've been watching and recording down any sign of a weakness that you have and they determined that I am it. They are going to kill me in front of you to weaken you so they can use the sword to cut your head off, dragon scales or not."

Fury filled his features, his eyes shifting between his human, dragon, and wolf ones quickly before returning to his blue human ones. "We're not going to let that happen." He pulled me out of his mom's hold and tilted my chin up so that we both sat on our knees, looking into each other's eyes. "You're not a weakness, Ember. You're going to stay at my side and we're going to protect each other, our entire pack. No more splitting the party, right? Always together."

"Together," I said and nodded. "No matter what, I'm not going to let them kill you. I'm not going to let them get what they want." I was going to find my parents and end this. Without them pulling the strings, we might be able to cause enough disorder among the H.E. to wipe them out.

He smiled. "There's my girl."

"Now, what's our next move?" Jolie asked.

My part done, I ended up sitting on Branson's lap sideways, curled up with my head on his shoulder, while everyone else talked and discussed plans.

Even with Branson being the largest of them, it wasn't fully comfortable since my legs either had to be tucked up or hanging over the side of the chair. So, I shifted into my rabbit form and curled into a little ball. He gently stroked my fur and I quickly fell asleep.

When I woke up, I was in Caleb's bed between Riddick and Caleb, in my human form wearing just my bra and underwear. Caleb had an arm beneath my head, under my pillow sleeping on his back and Riddick had an arm draped across my stomach laying on his side facing me.

Rolling onto my back jostled them enough to wake them up.

Caleb cracked an eye open, rolled over to face me, and pressed a light kiss to my cheek. "Morning," he mumbled, voice deep with sleep.

"Morning," I whispered back.

Riddick purred and nuzzled closer to me, his nose rubbing against my neck. "Sleepy," he whispered.

Taking his hand on my stomach, I pushed it down until he cupped me between my legs. "Still sleepy?" I asked.

His fingers curled around me and he moaned, pulled his hand up, and slid it back down under my underwear until he slid them between my folds.

"Yes," I breathed.

Caleb kissed and nipped at my shoulder, gently massaging my breasts through my bra.

Reaching down, I gripped his erection through his boxers. His hips arched and he let out a shuddering breath.

Riddick stroked his fingers back and forth quickly across my clit as he kissed the other shoulder.

"How do you want us?" Caleb asked.

"I want you to eat me while I give Riddick head," I answered.

Caleb kissed me and nodded. "As you wish."

Riddick withdrew his hand and both removed their boxers.

Staring at the two glorious males, prime specimens, I pinched my arm to confirm I wasn't dreaming.

Caleb pulled my underwear off and tapped me. "Riddick, on your back. Ember, on your hands and knees."

I rolled over, getting into the position he wanted so that I could take Riddick into my mouth while Caleb laid down on his back, scooting up until his head was beneath my hips. Pulling my hips down, he licked me and flicked his tongue across my clit.

Bending down, I sucked Riddick until he hit the back of my throat, then raised back up until he popped out of my mouth.

Riddick moaned, reached down, and slid his hand into my hair, guiding me down and up gently.

Caleb sucked on my clit, making me moan around Riddick, which made him moan, too.

I wanted faster, more.

"Ride his face and make yourself come," Riddick ordered me.

He wasn't normally the domineering one in the bedroom, but hearing him order me made me even hornier. I did as he said, moving my hips and riding Caleb's face in the way I wanted. Caleb reached up and cupped my breasts, squeezing and pinching my nipples.

"Relax your throat," Riddick ordered. I did. He purred, "Good girl."

Fuck. I shuddered in a good way and just as I came, Riddick did as well.

Sitting up, I wiped my mouth with the back of my hand and smiled at him as he panted.

Caleb slid out from under me, got onto his knees behind me, and thrust into me. Grabbing my neck gently, he pulled me up so I was on my knees with my back pressed to his chest, and he kept his hand on my throat as he thrust into me faster and harder. His thumb brushed across my jaw and he said, "I want to see your face as you come. It's so hot. You're so hot." He gripped the left side of my hip with his free hand and growled. "So beautiful."

I reached back and stroked a hand down his face. "How did I get so lucky to have such handsome men pleasuring me?"

"Come for me, Ember," Caleb ordered me. "Let me see that face of bliss."

His hips moved faster and I screamed his name as I came.

He smiled. "That's my girl."

Riddick got off the bed, but when he came back, he had a purple rope in his hands. "Do you trust us, Ember?" he asked.

I eyed the rope nervously, but nodded. "I trust you."

Caleb pulled out of me and they instructed me to lie on the bed on my back. "We'll start slow and easy," he whispered as Riddick tied my wrists together and up over my head, securing them to one of the bedposts. Once my arms were secured, Caleb spread my legs and licked his lips.

Riddick stroked his hand down one of my arms, traced his fingertips down my side, and back up. "Just say stop if it's too much, okay?"

I nodded.

"Tell us, Ember, what's something you like about us both?" Caleb asked as he climbed onto the bed on his knees and stroked himself while looking down at me.

"You're handsome," I said to Caleb. Turning my head to look at Riddick to my left I said, "You're beautiful."

"An okay answer," Riddick said, leaned forward, and sucked my nipple into his mouth, making me arch up.

"What's something you don't like about us?" Caleb asked.

"You're stubborn," I said breathlessly as Riddick continued to suck and swirl his tongue around my nipple.

Caleb smiled, leaned forward, and put a single finger inside of me, stroking slowly.

Riddick leaned back, hard again and stroking himself. "What's something we do that makes you feel good?"

"This feels pretty good," I said.

Caleb removed his finger. "Answer properly or you lose your rewards."

This was not what I had expected when they brought the rope out, but I still wanted to play along.

"When you hear my stomach growl and make me food without me asking, it feels good to know you are paying attention and care," I answered.

"That was a good answer," Caleb praised and slid two fingers inside of me, pumping faster than he had been before.

Riddick leaned down and gave me a long, deep kiss, our tongues dancing together.

"What's something you wish we did more of?" Caleb asked as he continued to stroke me, but slowed just a bit.

I was about to orgasm, so close that I could hardly think. Riddick ended our kiss so I could answer, kissing along my upper chest. "Um, included me in more of the hybrid research."

"What do you mean?" Riddick asked.

"I don't know how you find the hybrids," I explained and licked my lips.

"Okay," Caleb said with a nod. He curled his fingers slightly and asked, "How close are you, Ember?"

"Really close," I breathed.

He pulled his fingers out and Riddick stepped back as well.

"Last question and we'll give you the orgasm you want," Caleb promised.

"Okay," I nodded and tugged on the rope on my wrists.

Caleb put a condom on, arched my hips up, and pressed

the tip of his dick against my entrance. I tried to wiggle, but he held me still. "What's the thing you're scared of the most?"

My brows furrowed and I frowned. "What?"

Riddick pinched my nipple lightly. "You heard the question. What are you most terrified of?"

Caleb pressed in just a bit, stretching me open.

I didn't want to say it. I didn't want to admit it out loud to them.

Caleb started to pull back, but I said, "Fine!"

They both waited.

"I'm terrified of losing you, of being abandoned by you just like I've been dropped by two sets of parents. I'm scared this weird connection is the only thing keeping you here and that you don't want to mate with me."

Caleb's eyes widened slightly and he pushed into me, stretching me and making me moan. He thrust into me hard and fast, making me come twice before he came, pulled out, and Riddick took his place between my legs.

Caleb untied my wrists, and while Riddick fucked me, Caleb kissed me.

I came three more times before Riddick grunted and found his own release.

After throwing their condoms away, they spooned me on each side, stroking my body and kissing my face, neck, and shoulders. Pure boneless bliss had me smiling as I enjoyed their attention. Confessing all these things had take some weight off of my shoulders.

"Thank you," Caleb whispered.

Chuckling, I asked, "Shouldn't I be saying that?"

"I love you, Ember," Caleb whispered.

I sucked in a breath and looked at him, but he put a hand over my mouth. "Don't say anything. I know your life has caused insecurities and I thought you might have these fears, but just so you know, it's not the connection that makes me love the way you smile or the way your nose crinkles when you're annoyed."

"We love you because of who you are," Riddick whispered and kissed my temple. "I love you, Ember, because you are a beautiful, sweet, strong, and amazing person. I love you because you throw yourself into training to learn to protect others. Because you take the time to say goodnight to each of us, even if we aren't in the same room, before you go to bed."

"Mating must be decided on by all people and it's not something we've discussed with Branson and Triston yet," Caleb said.

"We know things haven't been the easiest and this is hardly the courting environment we wanted to experience with a potential mate, but we're trying our best," Riddick said.

Caleb kissed my forehead and said, "Okay, enough seriousness. Let's shower and then get breakfast."

He removed his hand and both slid out of the bed, leaving me blinking after them.

They ... loved me.

CHAPTER
EIGHTEEN

"You have to swear you won't tell anyone else about what you're about to participate in," Jolie said to Leona as we stood in Leona's backyard.

"I do not like this, but I will swear not to tell anyone as long as it's not something that is going to kill one of you," Leona replied.

Jolie shrugged. "Close enough." She turned and nodded at me. "Go ahead."

Centering myself, I opened a portal beneath Leona and one beneath Jolie to send them to the front yard.

Leona's eyes widened and she gasped.

Dropping them through it, I sealed it once they were through. My legs wobbled and heart pounded from the amount of magic I had used. Taking a shuddering breath, I jogged around the house to see Leona staring up at the sky.

"Great job!" Jolie praised. "How did it feel to open it, but hold us from falling through right away?"

"It was much easier this time. Now that I know to use

telekinesis for holding you while the portal opens, my mind is able to compartmentalize them," I answered as I slowed my heart and breathing, the magic depletion much stronger now that I had done two portals. I had to increase my stamina, to make sure I could do it for four portals.

"You ... opened a portal and sent me to the front yard," Leona whispered. She lowered her head to look at me. "Why is this a secret?"

"Because it causes a huge magic strain and is our ace up the sleeve to get everyone to safety," Jolie answered.

"And because Caleb won't like it," Leona added with a soft, knowing smile.

We both nodded.

Stepping up to Leona, I took her hands in mine and said, "I'd like your permission to have the portals open to here."

Her eyes opened a second, but then she smiled and squeezed my hands. "Permission granted. Just try to avoid letting enemies go through the portals, too."

"I will only send our people through," I promised with a nod. "I can use my telekinesis to hold them back long enough for the portal to close."

"Well, that's the plan, anyway," Jolie said. "Can we practice again?"

"Yeah, now that I am prepared for what we're doing," Leona said with a shake of her head. "Warn me next time, you brats."

"Hey, I'm going to drop you through a portal," I said, opened the portal beneath her feet, and dropped her into the backyard.

She yelped as she fell and yelled from the backyard, "Bitch!"

Jolie bent over, howling with laughter, and tears falling down her face. I did the same to her, earning a, "Fuck," as she fell and laughter from Leona.

Walking around the house, a huge smile on my face, I knew today was going to be a good day.

"This bitch," Jolie said and wiped her eyes.

"So, answer me this," Leona said as she stared down at the portal opening that I had just created. "When are you going to admit you are in love with those boys?"

I made Jolie fall through her portal first so she couldn't hear me reply, "When all four confirm they have feelings."

"Wait, who confessed?" she asked as she fell through.

Instead of walking around the house again, I teleported myself to them. "Let's talk about something else," I mumbled.

"One of them confessed in what way?" Jolie asked. "That they love you or that they want to take you as their mate?"

"Those are definitely two different confessions," Leona agreed with a nod.

"Two of them confessed both," I admitted. "Now, I've answered your questions, so let's get back to portals."

"Wait!" they both shouted.

"What did you say back?"

"They didn't let me respond," I grumbled. "One had a hand over my mouth to keep me from replying."

"Details, girl, details!" Leona shouted. "How did this come about?"

"Funny you should use that phrasing," I whispered, my

cheeks heating. This was not a conversation I wanted to have with Jolie present.

"Who was it? Was it Triston and Caleb?" Leona asked.

"I'm not going to tell you who it was," I said and folded my arms across my chest. "All you get to know is two of them said they love me and want to mate with me, but since they hadn't discussed it all together, they couldn't say how the other two feel."

"Have you told any of them that you love them?" Jolie asked.

"No."

"Why not?" Leona asked.

Creating two more portals, I sent them to the backyard again.

I sighed and yelled, "Because I'm a chicken!"

"No, you're a rabbit who can apparently create portals," Nico said behind me.

"Oh, shit. Busted!" Jolie yelled from the backyard.

Turning around, I smiled nervously. "Um, hi."

He folded his arms across his chest. "So, this is what you two have been up to in secret, huh?"

Jolie and Leona jogged over to us.

"Yes, I've been trying to learn a spell that I could use in the worst case scenario," I answered. "Are you mad?"

He looked at Jolie. "Why didn't you ask me?"

"Because you would rat us out to Caleb," Jolie replied. "Or to one of the others who would rat us out."

"Use one on me," he ordered me.

I held up a hand. "Let me finish catching my breath."

"How many have you created today?" he asked.

Jolie frowned. "Like a dozen."

His eyes widened. "How long have you been practicing behind our backs?"

Magic ready again, I created the portal and used my telekinesis to hold him above it. Then, I did the same to both Leona and Jolie. "Long enough that I can do this." I dropped all of them through the portals.

Nico looked up at me through the portal and I closed all three.

He teleported back to me and smiled wide. "It's been a long time since I've met someone who surprises me as often as you do, Ember. That was impressive. Now, I want you to do it while in warrior form."

"Trying to get her to deplete her magic faster?" Leona asked.

Nico shook his head, his hair, a bit shaggier than usual since he hadn't gotten it trimmed, flopping from side to side as he did. "No, I'm trying to ensure that she's able to fight after she uses them, in case others go through the portals with them. And, this time you are going to use it on all of us, including yourself. The only way I won't rat you out is if you confirm that you're going to use it for all of you."

"That's a lot of magic to use," I whispered nervously. That meant he wanted me to create five portals while in my warrior form and use telekinesis to keep the enemies from going through.

"You're already doing great," he praised. "It will just take practice and expanding your magic stamina."

"What if I don't have enough magic?" I asked. There were always limits to people's magic power.

"Then you'll know your limit ahead of a battle and won't be blindsided when the time comes to use this spell, and you'll have a plan for alternative escape. Now, create four portals, hold us all above them, and drop us after a count of three."

Hours of practice later, I lay on the grass, gasping for breath and covered in sweat.

"Well done," Nico praised and sat on the grass beside me. "Is this your plan if they manage to grab Caleb to try to decapitate him like they said they were going to?"

I nodded. "Yeah."

"Caleb sent me to check on you because he was worried Jolie was teaching you something dangerous and that's why you keep avoiding answering his questions, by the way. So, you might need to get prepared to answer him truthfully."

"I was planning to tell him soon," I admitted. "To show him that I can get us to safety so he won't try to keep me at home next fight we go to."

Nico chuckled. "Smart girl."

"How are my adoptive parents, a couple of humans, able to avoid us so easily?" I asked.

"They have some powerful people on their side," he said, scowling. "They are keeping them safe and hidden from us."

"I hate this," I whispered.

"Learning new powers?" he asked and arched a brow.

"Needing to learn a failsafe because people want to kill us."

"Welcome to the life of a royal," he said and chuckled softly. "If it's any consolation, I think you've adapted pretty well from being a hermit."

Smiling, I said, "Thanks, Nico."

"Recouped enough to try again?" he asked and climbed to his feet, a hand down to help me up.

Caleb called my name from the house as he walked through.

"Maybe not," I said and flinched.

"Oh, no. This is perfect," Nico said. "Jolie! Leona! Come here please."

Caleb jogged over and kissed my cheek. "Hey, beautiful. What's going on?"

"Practice," I answered and smiled up at him.

"Oh? The mysterious practice you've been doing with Mom?"

I nodded.

"Okay, this time, you're going to create five, got it?" Nico said. "This is the ultimate test, right?"

"Right," I agreed. This is what I would need to do in the future.

"Jolie, go about twenty yards that way. Caleb, go ten yards in the other direction. Leona, stay where you are. I'm going to go over here." Nico instructed everyone where to go, so that we were all spread out in various distances. Once in place, he gave me a thumbs up.

I smiled at Caleb and said, "Surprise!" Opening all the portals, I dropped us all through and out to the front yard.

Nico and I ended up falling almost on top of each other, but he reached out and steadied me. I dropped to my hands and knees, gasping for breath. Five portals was definitely my limit. It felt like my heart was going to explode.

Caleb looked up at the still open portal and lowered his

gaze until he looked at me for a second before turning to his mother. "What the fuck, Mom?"

"Caleb," Nico warned.

"You're teaching her to send us away? To send us to safety!" He growled and turned to his dad. "And you're helping them?"

"It's always important to have an escape plan, Caleb. There are some battles that you cannot win," Nico reminded him.

"This is why we didn't tell you," I said angrily. "Because we knew you would overreact."

"Your heart is about to burst and you're wondering why I wouldn't want you to do this?"

Shooting up to my feet, I turned and glared at him. "I'm not going to let you die! I don't care if you think it's cowardly or if it drains me of magic at the end. If I can save you, I'm going to."

"Save me or save us?" he asked. "Are you going to sacrifice yourself? Is that what you think you're supposed to do?"

"I made five portals," I reminded him. "I plan to use one on myself, too. I don't want to die any more than you do."

"Everyone, take a deep breath," Leona ordered us and used her magic to relax us all a bit.

Caleb glared at her and stomped over to the SUV he'd come in where Ezio was leaned and watching us.

"Well, that went better than I expected," Jolie said and slung her arm around my shoulders. "Don't worry, he'll get over it."

"At least you are capable of five portals as your max, since that's what you'll need to escape," Nico said. "Don't worry, we'll talk to him and calm him down."

"Let's head home," Jolie said and tugged me towards the car. "You've done a lot of work today and deserve to rest."

I felt like resting wasn't going to be an option with Caleb so upset and likely to cause the others to get upset when he told them.

"Can't we have a girls' night?" I asked.

Leona laughed and shook her head. "Welcome to the trials and tribulations we warned you about."

I sighed and stepped away from Jolie. "I'm not riding in that car with him. I'll see you at home." I teleported to my bedroom and flopped onto my bed.

CHAPTER

NINETEEN

Two days' later, all four continued to sulk and ignore me. Caleb's fathers tried to talk to them, but the four ignored all of their advice.

Jolie had me help her with the planning of an upcoming event, a birthday party for Dan, that was going to be huge and extravagant and require formal attire. It was distraction enough for the day, but in the evening, I lay in my room alone, feeling cold and lonely.

That third night, I had had enough. Stomping down the hallway, I pounded my fist on Caleb's door.

He opened it and folded his arms across his chest and leaned against his doorjamb.

"You're a jerk!" I shouted at him. "You've isolated me for three fucking nights! I can't stand it any longer." My chest heaved and my hands clenched into fists at my side as I stared at him.

His eyes widened and he dropped his arms. "Em –"

"You told me to tell you when I need something, well I

need you to pull your head out of your ass and stop treating me like I did something wrong. I've learned a spell that will save us. A spell that I won't use lightly. I did something good. Something your parents have praised me for, but what have you done? You've shut me out, ignored me, and left me alone for three nights. Do you realize how embarrassing it is for me to come here to admit that I need a fucking hug? That I feel like my skin is crawling with ants because none of you has so much as held my hand or kissed my cheek? What if we got attacked tonight? What if the mage my dad ordered to murder me did it tonight? Would you feel fine knowing how you've treated me? I just want a fucking hug." Tears spilled down my cheeks and I wiped them away roughly.

He pulled me into a hug and I sobbed against his chest at the instant relief it gave me. "I'm sorry. I'm a fucking idiot. I'm sorry, Ember."

Doors opened and then all four of them were touching me and hugging me between them.

The floodgates opened and I sobbed between them.

They all apologized, but I was still mad and hurt.

"We're idiots," Triston whispered. "We know you didn't do anything wrong. Learning spells for safety are not wrong."

"We're just worried, that's all," Branson added. "You always use your magic up and this type of spell is very draining."

"We're sorry, Ember. We shouldn't have isolated you," Riddick said and kissed the top of my head.

"Come on, let's go downstairs and watch a movie together and cuddle on the couch, okay?" Caleb suggested.

Nodding, I let them lead me down to the living room.

Jolie watched us go by and her eyes narrowed. "Why are you crying?"

"It's okay, Mom," Caleb said.

"Oh, did you finally pull your heads out of your asses?" she asked and put her hands on her hips.

"Yes," Riddick answered.

"No, Ember yanked them out for us," Triston replied and winked at me.

She scoffed. "Figures. You four are even more stubborn than my mates, which is quite a freakin' feat. Triston, come help me finish making snacks so you can take them with you."

"Yes, ma'am," he said with a nod, kissed my cheek, and followed her to the kitchen.

We sat on the couch and Caleb ran his fingers through my hair. "I'm proud of you, Ember."

"Why?" I asked. "I just screamed at you all."

"Because you finally told us what you wanted without us asking first and because you stood up for yourself. I really am sorry we tormented you. That wasn't my intent." He wrapped his arms around me and squeezed tightly. "I promise we won't do that ever again, okay?"

I nodded and swallowed hard, not able to speak.

"Shall we watch the romcom you added to the watchlist yesterday?" Branson asked.

"What about that new action movie instead?" I suggested. I wasn't really in the mood for relationship drama, even one with laughs and a happy ending.

"Sounds good to me," Riddick agreed.

Nico ran down the stairs, a staff in hand, and shouted, "Barrier breach!"

Our relaxing evening was shattered and we all shot to our feet.

"Stay inside," Rhys ordered us as he and Deryn headed for the front door.

Jolie and Triston ran out from the kitchen and she pointed at us. "Stay."

Caleb rolled his eyes. "I swear they still view me as five sometimes."

A few minutes later, they returned, scowling, but without any injuries.

"What happened?" I asked.

"A werewolf sent by Dan," Rhys answered.

"He's a newer pack member," Deryn said with a shrug of his shoulder.

"Is Dan okay?" I asked.

Nico and Fox walked in carrying several pizza boxes.

"It was just a delivery," Deryn explained. "He just forgot to text us to let us know that it was being sent over. I swear he's getting senile in his old age."

"Be nice to your dad," Jolie said and shook her head. "You know he's been busy."

"Well, looks like the snacks we were gathering aren't necessary anymore," Triston said with a chuckle.

"But those drinks are definitely necessary!" Jolie yelled. "Help me grab the beers, Ember."

I followed and she hugged me tightly. "Things good now?"

"They're better." I cringed as I added, "I yelled at them."

She smiled and squeezed me. "That'a girl. Put them in their place. It's necessary from time to time."

Laughing, I shook my head. "Well, hopefully there won't be need of that in the future." Yelling definitely wasn't something I wanted to be common for us.

She scoffed. "You clearly don't know those boys."

I squeezed her back and said, "I appreciate your support. Honestly, I was really close to coming to you for help, but reminded myself that I need to take care of things on my own. That ended with me yelling and ultimately things turned out alright, but I need to figure out a healthy way to address them in the future."

"That is a very tall order, but I appreciate your willingness to try to find it," she said.

We made it into the kitchen, grabbed the cases of beer in the fridge, and carried them out to the living room where everyone was spread out on the couches and had started eating.

Jolie handed me a slice of pizza as the guys started opening their beers.

"This is really good pizza," Branson praised.

Deryn nodded. "Dad spent a lot of money and time finding the best recipes that he could to craft the best recipes and best pizzas available."

"We were also guinea pigs a lot for this," Fox said and scowled. "The first pizzas were awful."

"Some were super thick, cakey almost," Rhys said with his brows furrowed. "These are so much better."

"Remember the pizza he made where he put the toppings

under the cheese?" Deryn asked and shook his head. "Everyone hated it."

"People are used to things in a certain way and the toppings being on top of the cheese is one of them," Fox said. "Although, I personally liked it being under the cheese as it kept it from falling off as you ate it."

"Right?" Nico yelled. "It was perfect for parties where people were drunk and ended up dropping toppings on the floor."

Take a seat on the arm of the couch next to Branson, I listened silently, I enjoyed hearing about the strange and random issues they had encountered as they grew up, things that still transcended time. I wished this had been more of my life.

"What are your favorite pizza toppings, Ember?" Fox asked.

"Salami, olives, and pineapple," I answered.

Deryn and Rhys groaned.

"Pineapple, really?" Deryn asked. "It does not belong on pizza."

I rolled my eyes.

"It is a staple pizza topping," Caleb countered. "Why else would Papa Dan offer it?"

"Because weirdos, like Ember apparently, like it," Rhys said and shook his head.

"You like sweet and sour chicken which has pineapple, but you're going to say suddenly, sweet and sour foods don't go together? Nah. You're just being ridiculous," I countered and finished eating my slice.

"She's got a point," Jolie said and shrugged. "I don't like

pineapple on my pizza, but she's got a point about the tastes."

"Don't help her and her gross tendencies," Riddick said. "It's weird."

"You're weird," I countered, obviously not providing a good argument.

"And yet, you still spend your time with me," Riddick said with a smirk.

"What's your ideal pizza?" I asked Caleb. "Let me guess, all meat?"

He opened his mouth and shut it. "What's wrong with all meat?"

Everyone laughed.

"Nothing, handsome. Absolutely nothing," I crooned.

"Favorite dessert?" Fox asked as he looked at us.

Clearly, they all knew their favorite desserts already.

"I don't have a single favorite," I admitted. "I like cheesecakes, chocolate chip cookies, ice cream, and more."

"What about birthday cake flavored ice cream with chocolate covered cheesecake chunks?" Rhys asked.

I gasped. "That sounds amazing."

"That does sound amazing," Jolie agreed.

"What's your favorite dessert?" I asked Riddick.

"Tiramisu," Caleb answered.

Riddick shook his head. "No, it's not."

Caleb scowled. "What? That's always been your favorite dessert."

"No, I like truffles," Riddick said. "You always get it confused."

"Oh," Caleb said, drawing the word out. "You're right."

Riddick rolled his eyes. "Yes, I'm sure I got my favorite dessert right."

Several of the guys laughed.

"Branson's favorite is ... strawberry cobbler, right?" I remembered making it once for him.

He nodded. "Yep." He turned to Triston next to him and asked, "What about you?"

Triston shrugged. "I like most things sweet, like Ember." He winked at me and I felt my face heat up.

"Caleb's is brownies," Fox said.

Caleb scoffed. "No, it's not, Dad."

"What?" Fox gasped. "Since when?"

"Just because I like brownies doesn't mean it's my favorite."

"Red velvet cake," Deryn said.

Caleb shook his head. "Nope, wrong again."

"Lemon bars?" Rhys said, but it was definitely a question.

Caleb sighed. "My own parents don't know my favorite dessert. Wow. I'm hurt."

"Carrot cake," Jolie said.

Caleb pointed at her. "Mom for the win!"

My nose scrunched at the thought of carrot cake. "Ew."

Caleb frowned at me. "What? You don't like carrot cake?"

I shook my head. "No, it's gross."

He smiled and said, "I'm pretty sure rabbits like carrot."

My eyes narrowed and I said, "Carrots are delicious, but they don't belong in sweets."

"I think you just hurt the soul of every rabbit in existence with that statement," Caleb teased.

"What is your favorite present to ever receive?" Triston

asked Branson.

Branson frowned as he thought about it a minute. "My nana made me a blanket one year, she guessed I was going to get big since I was a bear, so she made it extra big. It kept me warm and was super soft."

A handmade blanket? How sweet! The closest thing I got was the trinkets Beatrice brought me.

"I think mine was the video game console my dad bought for us to play games together," Triston said. "We spent many Saturday mornings playing games. What about you, Riddick?"

"The bow," he answered. Jolie and her mates all smiled. When Riddick realized we didn't know what he meant, he added, "They bought me a bow the second year after I met Caleb."

"They'd started watching a TV show and the main character used a bow and he kept running around pretending to use one," Fox said. "So, we bought him one."

"He immediately ran out of the house and started using it," Rhys said with a soft chuckle. "Stayed outside the rest of the evening trying it out."

I chuckled, picturing a small Riddick running around in the woods, shooting his bow.

"Caleb, what's yours?" Riddick asked him, the tips of his ears red.

"That's a hard one," Caleb said. "I don't think I have a favorite. What about you, Ember?"

I shrugged. "I don't really remember the gifts I got."

"You didn't celebrate with your patients or Branson or anyone?" Jolie asked.

"I only knew Branson a couple of months before you guys. I was more worried about treating my patients than gifts. I guess, the medical backpack I bought myself, if that counts. Or the shiny things Beatrice brought me when she would find things in the river or while she was out flying around."

Caleb scowled and Jolie smiled sadly.

"Beatrice brought you gifts often?" Triston asked.

I nodded. "When she realized that I liked them, she started doing it more and more and I started giving her gifts, too. Like a braided piece of twine that she incorporated into her nest. I also took some of the shiny things she brought me and decorated the outside of her nest with them, which made her really happy."

"And now she brings Dad things and practically lives on his shoulder," Deryn said. "He's become pretty fond of her. Even built her a nest in his house."

That made me really happy to hear. "That's so sweet."

"Yeah, Dan's a big softy," Jolie said with a smile.

They talked a bit more about gifts and things they'd received and then, as often happened, we played video games.

There was something about the games that had a way of bringing us all together, even if we shouted occasionally when we lost or someone played dirty. This, this was the type of gathering I wanted to participate in often. One with smiles, laughter, and true enjoyment of each other's presence.

This was what I had craved for so long and I was going to do everything in my power to protect it.

CHAPTER
TWENTY

"*Ember!*" Beatrice cawed as she flew from Dan's shoulder to mine and rubbed her face along my cheek. "*You came back.*"

I stroked her feathers and said, "Of course I came back. How are you doing?"

"*Big nest!*" she shouted and cawed loudly. "*He gave me a big big nest. Lots of shiny.*"

"Oh," I said and looked at Dan who was hugging Caleb. "You gave her a nest and shiny things?"

He smiled. "I did some research on what ravens like and tested a few things out to see what she liked the best. It seems I did a good job if she's telling you about it." He sighed. "I still wish I could talk to her."

"Beatrice, is there anything you want me to tell Dan?" I asked her. I could play interpreter for her.

"Oh! Tell him I like the nuts more than berries," she said and bobbed her beak up and down.

"She said she likes nuts more than berries," I repeated.

Dan chuckled. "I was starting to figure that out, but thank you, that's helpful."

"Papa, is it okay if I take Ember to the market?" Caleb asked.

Dan scowled. "Why are you asking me, son? Of course, you can. Ember's welcome here whenever she wants."

My eyes widened. "I'm not a werewolf, though."

"I didn't say you were." He winked. "Branson, come help me in the house."

Branson brushed a hand along my back as he passed. "Yes, sir."

"Bye, Ember," Beatrice said and flew over to Dan's shoulder. He pulled something from his shirt pocket and fed it to her.

It was great to see her so happy.

"Come on," Caleb said and linked our hands together. "The market is great. You're going to love it." We headed around the house and deeper into the Den, as they called the werewolf area. It was basically its own city with houses, shops, forest, schools, and everything they could want.

Triston walked on my right side, humming a song, and Riddick trailed behind us.

As we walked by people, they bowed their heads to Caleb, recognizing him as their superior in the pack, and prince.

"Caleb!" a woman shouted and waved as she ran forward. She looked to be about our age, had a slim figure, but muscular arms, wore a cute sundress with strawberries on it and had her hair up in a ponytail with the ends of her hair curled and bouncing behind her.

"Hello, Priscilla," Caleb greeted her. "How's your brother?"

She frowned. "He's fine." Her eyes dropped to our joined hands and her entire body stiffened. She raised her eyes up to mine and her lip twitched in a snarl. "So, the rumors are true. You're courting a non-wolf."

"Ember, this is Priscilla. Priscilla, this is Ember. Priscilla's brother Larry and I have been friends since elementary school," Caleb explained.

She scowled, but quickly smiled and said, "Yes, Caleb and I have known each other our entire lives. If you're not busy later –"

"Sorry, I'm taking Ember to the market," Caleb said. "I'll catch up with you some other time. Tell your brother I said hi and to call me."

Her smile quivered. "Right."

Caleb raised his hand in the air as we walked away.

"Wow, that was cold," I whispered.

"Ice cold," Triston agreed.

"What?" Caleb asked and looked over at us with an arched brow.

"You friend zoned her so hard and told her she was just your friend's little sister. No wonder you've never dated before." Triston shook his head.

"I've dated before," Caleb argued.

"No, you've gone on dates, but you weren't ever interested or paid attention to them in that way," Riddick said from behind us. "Just because you've gone through the motions doesn't mean it really counts."

"What are you talking about?" Caleb asked.

"Remember the double date we went on with the twins?" Riddick asked.

"Yeah."

"You barely talked to them and spent more time on your phone, more grunting in response than answering with words," Riddick said and shook his head. "Those girls walked with their heads down as they left."

"You were the one who suggested we accept their offer," Caleb said and growled softly. "I didn't want to go with them anyway. They were whiny."

"They were trying to play towards your alpha instincts," Riddick said and laughed. "Man, you are hopeless. I don't know how you changed so drastically when it comes to Ember, but I'm glad because otherwise we'd all be doing double duty to make up for you."

"Whatever," Caleb grumbled.

We made it away from the houses and into an area that was grassy with wooden stalls on each side and each stall had a vendor with different items. There were also several people selling drinks and food.

"Oh, my gosh, this is so adorable!" I gasped. "It's just like the movies of the small towns."

I visited every single stall, looking at the various hand-crafted items. "I need to come back here when I have more money," I said.

"See something you like?" a tall man with thick grey hair braided on each side at his temple asked from behind the stall I was in front of.

I nodded. "Everything is lovely, but this is exquisite." Gingerly, I picked up a wooden, hand carved, howling wolf with trees carved into the side of it. The wolf was so well done.

"Of course you picked that one," Riddick said and scoffed while Caleb snickered behind me.

"What?" I asked.

"That piece is of our prince here," the man said. "I carved this in honor of his eighteenth birthday."

The one item I had picked up had been a replica of Caleb. What were the odds?

I set it back down and chuckled in embarrassment. "Ah, well, um, it's very well done. I love the details and the trees." Moving away quickly, I headed to another stall, ignoring the still snickering Caleb.

"What's your favorite here?" Triston asked as he leaned over next to me, inspecting the wooden boxes with various carvings. They were somewhat small, but seemed like they were used for storing jewelry or trinkets. The carvings ranged from scenery, to animals, to hearts with ornate knot-work around the edges.

"This one I think is my favorite," I said and pointed at a box with a heart in the center and an infinity symbol through the middle. The front had a bright purple gemstone embedded in it.

"That one is gorgeous," Triston agreed with a nod. He turned and looked away then asked, "Do you want a snack? I'm starting to get hungry."

I nodded. "A snack sounds good."

He took some money out of his pocket and asked, "Can you get four of the spiral meat sticks for us?"

"Oh, sure," I said, took the money and walked over to get

in line. Luckily, there were only two other people waiting in front of me.

The woman right in front of me turned around and scowled down at me. She appeared to be slightly younger than me, but was several inches taller and way bustier than me, a fact seen by her low-cut shirt. "Who are you?"

I smiled. "I'm Ember. I'm visiting with Prince Caleb today."

Her eyes narrowed. "You? You're the one he's been seen with? How could he possibly be interested in you? You reek and you're obviously not an alpha. A dominant alpha like him should be with a female of the same caliber." She scoffed and flipped her hair over her shoulder as she turned back around. "What a waste."

"I didn't realize female wolves were catty. Seems a bit of a contradiction," I snapped back.

She spun back around, lip lifted in a snarl, and growled at me. "What did you say?"

I put a hand on my hip and cocked it to the side. "You heard me. The reason he's not interested in you is because dominance doesn't matter. What matters is not being a conceited bitch."

She raised her fist and I flicked my finger up, shooting roots out of the ground to wind around her entire body and hold her still.

Everyone around us froze, turning to watch what was happening.

"I was nice to you, but you responded to that niceness with rude remarks. You don't know me. You have no idea what I'm like. You don't know if I'm powerful or not. You should remember that people aren't always what they seem. I may not be a wolf shifter, but I can still protect myself."

Caleb walked over, hands in his pockets, and asked, "Everything okay?"

I sent the roots back into the ground and she stumbled back several steps, bumping into the person at the front of the line. "Yeah, everything's great," I said and smiled at him.

He draped an arm around my shoulders and kissed the side of my head. "Glad to hear it. Oh, meat sticks. I love these."

The woman stormed off, face red, and hands clenched into fists at her side.

"Well, that's one way to introduce yourself to the pack," he whispered in my ear and laughed softly, nuzzling his nose against my neck.

Sighing, I shook my head. "Sorry, I overreacted. I should have just ignored her."

He shrugged. "I think you handled it fine. No blood was shed and the only thing that was lost was her dignity."

I noticed Riddick and Triston each had bags in their hands. "What are you guys buying?"

"Oh, just a few things for the apartment," he said.

"Hello, Your Highness," the seller greeted, distracting me from the other two and refocusing me on the delicious smelling food before us.

"Can we have four, please?" I requested and set the money Triston had given me on the counter.

"Make it eight," Caleb amended and set more money down.

"Right away," the man said and nodded, turning to grab

the meat from the grill. They were spiral cut meat with a wooden skewer pushed through the center and covered in seasoning.

"Thank you," I said as I took two of the skewers.

Caleb carried the other six and distributed them two each to Triston and Riddick who had walked over to join us.

Taking a bite, I immediately closed my eyes and moaned. It was seasoned to perfection! "So good," I whispered around the hot food in my mouth.

"This is delicious," Triston agreed.

"I need to learn to make this," I said and opened my eyes.

Caleb, Riddick, and Triston had all already consumed their sticks and tossed their skewers into the trash.

"I know how to cook them," Caleb said. "I just never think about making them."

"Dinner tonight," I said with a nod. "That's when you should make them."

He chuckled and looped his arm around my waist. "Anything for you."

"In that case, I would like a house with a wraparound porch, a porch swing on each side of the house, and a balcony that goes all the way around the top floor so everyone can walk out of their rooms and onto the balcony to hang out together," I joked as we continued down to look at more stalls.

"Noted," he said with a nod. "Do you want the first floor to be an open view with the kitchen and a huge living room slash dining room? We could put all the bedrooms upstairs."

"Oh, that sounds nice," I said. "Could we have a sunken

living room? You know, where you step down a few steps into it? I saw one on a television show and loved that idea."

"Fireplace in the center?" he asked.

"No, but maybe a shared bedroom upstairs with a large fireplace?" I suggested.

"So, individually bedrooms and one giant room that everyone could sleep in together?" he asked and looked down at me with a thoughtful expression.

My smile slipped. "Caleb, I was joking. I was just teasing you because you said anything."

He stepped in front of me, set his hands on my hips, and said, "I was being serious, Ember. Plus, I like hearing what you want. It'll make building our pack's house much easier."

"Our pack's house?" I asked, my voice a squeak.

He nodded. "You know, once we prove we're worthy of you and have the inevitable discussion about mating."

I swallowed hard. "Pretty sure I'm the one needing to prove her worth."

"Your existence is enough," he said, brushed his lips over mine, and turned to walk up to the next stall.

My face burned and my heart pounded in my chest. I shoved the meat stick into my mouth and ate it to distract myself.

TWENTY-ONE

"Caleb? Riddick? Triston? Branson?" I called as I walked through the seemingly empty house.

After our afternoon practice I had gone to shower and change, but when I came out, everyone was gone.

Fear grew in my chest, making me start to panic. Closing my eyes, I looked at Caleb's connection and started following it through the house. It led me out to the front door. I opened it and peeked outside, listening for sounds of fighting or danger. Hearing none, I continued tracking Caleb, walking across the grass and heading towards the woods.

Suddenly, his location changed and it led me back into the house.

Confused and worried, my brows furrowed as I walked inside of the house and towards the dining room.

"Caleb?" I called.

"In here," he called back from the dining room.

Exhaling in relief, I pushed open the door. "Thank goodness. I was starting to wo—"

"Happy birthday!" several voices shouted.

I froze and blinked at the crowded dining room where balloons, a banner, and bright table decorations were laid out. In the center stood a large three-tier cake with candles burning.

Tears sprang to my eyes and my hands went to my mouth.

Caleb, Branson, Triston, Riddick, Jolie and her mates, Leona and her mates, Dan, Katar, Kara, Emrys, Ezio, and Kieran all wore birthday hats and smiled at me.

"Uh oh, I warned you she might cry," Kara said.

Jolie rushed over, hugged me, and kissed each of my cheeks. "Happy birthday, Ember."

"How did you know?" I asked. "I'd forgotten."

"We had your birth certificate, remember?" Deryn reminded me.

"Your pack has been planning it for weeks," Kieran said as he walked over and hugged me. "Happy birthday, Em and Em."

I hugged him back. "Thank you for coming. How are you?"

He smiled. "I'm good. Thank you."

Caleb put a birthday hat on me, being sure not to snap the elastic band beneath my chin, and wiped beneath my eyes. "Happy birthday, beautiful." He kissed my cheek and whispered in my ear, "Great job tracking me. I had to run outside because you were getting too close to discovering us before they finished setting up."

Laughing softly, I turned and kissed his cheek. "Thank you."

"Come blow out the candles," Triston urged. "The wax is going to get all over the cake if you wait too long."

I walked over and looked at all of the smiling faces of people I had grown to know and care about over the past several months. People I considered an extended family. I smiled wide. "Thank you all for coming."

"Make a wish," Riddick said.

I shook my head and blew the candles out. "I don't have anything to wish for. I've got everything already."

Triston kissed my cheek. "Happy birthday, gorgeous."

"I'll cut the cake," Branson offered and with Riddick and Triston's help, they cut and passed out slices of cake.

I sat down in the chair at the head of the table and ate the delicious cake.

"Present time!" Caleb announced.

I frowned. "You didn't need to get me presents. You've all given me so much already."

"Nonsense," Leona said. "Everyone gets presents on their birthday. Mine first!"

Silverowl carried over a large rectangular box with a red ribbon around it. He smiled, set the box on the table before me, and said, "Happy birthday, Rubyhare Ember."

I untied the ribbon and lifted the lid, gasping at the gorgeous ruby red dress inside. "Oh, wow. Thank you so much."

"You're welcome," Leona said. "I saw it and knew it was meant for you."

"Mine next!" Jolie shouted and waved at Rhys.

Rhys grabbed a small white bag with silver tissue paper inside. He set it down on the table.

"This is from my pack," Jolie said. "We hope you like it."

"I'll love anything you give me," I said. "Even a shiny rock, as long as it doesn't explode."

Everyone laughed.

Pulling the tissue paper out carefully, I gasped when I saw a car key fob inside. "What ... what is this?"

"Your new car!" Jolie shouted. "It's in the garage. We didn't want you stumbling upon it when you were outside. We'll take you to see it after all the gifts are opened."

"Thank you!" I yelled, though my heart beat erratically and my brain whirred from being so stunned. I wasn't sure I'd ever been so stunned by a present.

"My turn," Triston said and put a wrapped box in front of me.

I opened it and found the pretty jewelry box I'd pointed out at the werewolf den. "Triston," I gasped, "thank you."

"Now you have a place to put the bracelet and other things we've bought you," he said.

"Me next," Riddick said.

His gift was a pair of ruby earrings.

He smiled. "I may have caught wind about Leona's gift."

"They're lovely," I said and stroked a finger down them.

"Okay, my turn," Caleb said and set a bag in front of me.

His smile looked a bit teasing and it made me worry as I opened it. My face grew hot and I groaned when I saw the wooden wolf sculpture.

Pulling it out, Triston and Riddick started laughing.

Dan asked, "You bought her a carving of yourself?"

"She picked it out when we were at the Den," Caleb said with a smug smile. "Said it was her favorite carving."

"It is really well done," I said and put it back in the bag. "Thank you, even if I am embarrassed."

He kissed my cheek and whispered in my ear, "It was just confirmation that you're meant to be mine."

Now my entire face was on fire.

"Here's mine," Kieran said and set a small bag in front of me.

Inside was a carving of a raven that looked exactly like Beatrice. "Oh, wow! Thank you, Kieran."

He smiled and said, "You're welcome."

"That's really good, did you do it?" Caleb asked him.

Kieran nodded. "Thank you."

"It looks just like Beatrice," Dan praised as he inspected it. "Do you sell these?"

Kieran shook his head. "It's just a hobby."

"You could make money doing this," Dan said. "Let's talk after."

Kieran's ears reddened and he nodded.

Turning back to me, Dan said, "So, the rest of the royals got you a combined gift. And it's actually a gift for your entire pack, not just you."

I looked at him curiously. "Oh?" What could it be?

Caleb looked just as surprised as me, so obviously he hadn't known.

Katar slid a large envelope down the table and Caleb caught it and opened it. He stared at the photo a second and then set it on the table so everyone could see it.

It was an aerial view of a forest.

"Thank you," I said, confused.

All of them laughed.

"What is it?" Caleb asked.

"An aerial view of your pack's territory," Emrys answered.

I gasped and looked at each of them. "You're serious?"

"Whoa," Branson breathed.

"Where?" Caleb asked and picked the picture up again, holding it tenderly like he might break it.

"To the east of Jinla, about twenty minutes. It's one hundred acres and we have one housing plot flattened and ready for you to build your first house, with utilities and a well all ready for you," Dan said. "The crew is ready to go flatten other areas for whatever hybrids join you."

I leapt out of my chair and hugged the large man, then made my way around to hug all of them. "Thank you." Just last week I had debated asking Dan about the possibility of us getting territory for our pack, not just our fivesome, but for all hybrids.

"Well, as King of the Hybrids, Caleb needs his own territory," Kara said. "And when you start building, I'll help you set up a healer's cabin."

Tears built in my eyes and I smiled at her. "That would be wonderful."

"Don't cry or I'm going to cry," Jolie said and fanned at her face.

"Come on, let's go see your new car," Riddick suggested.

Caleb stayed back to hug his grandparents and thank them, clearly much more emotional about the gift than me, as it had a completely different meaning for him.

My car was actually a silver SUV with tinted, bullet-proof windows. "It's perfect," I said with a nod. Exactly what a pack of hybrids who were constantly targeted needed.

"We're glad you like it," Fox said. "We argued about what to get you for several days."

Rhys laughed. "More like a week."

"I wanted to get you a sportscar, but we figured Caleb wouldn't like that," Deryn said.

"I suggested a truck," Nico said. "Since that's what you had before."

"That was practical when she lived in the woods, but not now," Jolie said and shook her head.

"You can see why we spent a bit deciding," Fox said and shook his head while smiling.

"I love it, thank you."

Jolie hugged me. "Good birthday?" she asked.

I nodded. "The best one I've ever had."

"The best one you've had yet," Triston countered and pulled me into a hug. "As long as we're with you, we're going to make sure each and every single one of them is better than the previous."

"As long as I'm not alone, it's a great birthday," I said. "I appreciate the thoughtful gifts, too."

"Want to play some games now?" Jolie asked.

"I'll even let you beat me at karting," Fox taunted.

"Oh, it's on!" I shouted. "I'm dethroning you today."

"Bring it on, birthday girl," he said and headed out of the garage.

The kings and Kara ended up staying and playing with us as well, which made it the most epic birthday ever. Watching Queen Kara of the Elves playing videogames against King

Emrys of the Dragons, yelling and growling at each other was hilarious. I laughed so hard I almost peed myself.

While everyone was watching the match, I walked to Caleb who stood against the back wall and hugged him. "Thank you."

He kissed the top of my head and said, "You're welcome, Ember."

Tilting my head back so I could look up into his eyes, I said, "You know why I didn't need a gift?"

"Hm?"

"Because I'm already the luckiest woman in the world." I squeezed him. "I've got you and the others. What else could I possibly want?"

He pulled out the picture and said, "How about a two-story house with a wraparound porch, a wraparound balcony, and a recessed living room?"

My eyes widened.

"And a secondary house is already being planned," he said.

"For who?"

"Me," Kieran said from behind me.

I turned around and he smiled. "I've always wanted to be part of a pack, but thought it wouldn't be possible. Now that I've met our king, how can I say no?"

Spinning back around, I looked up at Caleb. "You're serious?"

He nodded. "I am. Your speech the other night really hit me hard. There's never going to be a perfect time or right time for me to accept my role. Now is the perfect time for me to accept it and start making strides to have a place we can live our lives peacefully. Dad is going to help me set up wards and we'll ensure that any hybrid that wishes to join us will have a safe place to come to."

"This might be the greatest present of the night," I whispered.

He cupped my cheek and said, "None of this would be possible with you, my bunny queen."

"You cheated again!" Kara yelled at Katar. "What kind of king cheats?"

"One who refuses to let his wife beat him," Katar said with a chuckle.

"Like father like son," Jolie said and scoffed.

"I don't cheat! It's part of the game, so it's fair," Fox countered.

Caleb kissed me and said, "Happy birthday, Ember. Now, come get beaten by me."

"Challenge accepted," I said and smiled up at him, feeling a space within my heart that had felt empty start to fill.

"Me next," Branson said. "I'm going to beat Ember tonight. I can feel it."

"Oh, Branny Boy," I crooned, "you don't stand a chance, but you're welcome to try."

"Come on, Ember, show these boys who the best gamer is," Jolie cheered.

"My own mother rooting against me," Caleb said and shook his head.

"I think after this we should play that card game where you get to say less and less words and do boys versus girls," I said as I sat and took the controller from Kara.

"Yes!" Kara agreed. "I like this plan."

"You're still going to lose, darling," Katar said and kissed her cheek.

How had this, being surrounded by royalty and playing videogames together, become my life?

Whatever the reason, I was so happy and couldn't wait to see what the future had in store for us.

CHAPTER
TWENTY-TWO

"Try six portals," Caleb said after we stretched in preparation of our morning training sessions.

"I can't make the sixth one," I argued.

"Practice helps, remember? Just try."

I sighed, stood up from the grass, and created five portals on the grass where no one was standing.

Everyone watched, waiting to see what would happen.

A sixth one popped open and immediately shut.

Falling to my knees, I gasped for breath.

"What's going on?" Nico asked as he joined us in his sweats and t-shirt.

"She opened a sixth one, but it closed as soon as she opened it," Caleb said.

Nico set his hand on me and my breathing became easier. "She can't do six, Caleb. She needs to practice holding the five open longer before she tries to make the sixth. Opening a portal is much more taxing and draining than holding ones already created open."

I sat back and Nico patted my back. "Thanks," I said and wiped the dirt from my hands.

"We've got to get you to the point of being able to do six," he said softly and walked away, headed towards Rhys to start his sparring practice.

"Did something happen?" Nico asked me softly.

"Your guess is as good as mine," I said and shrugged. "He woke up this morning growling. I think maybe a bad dream?"

Nico sighed and ran a hand down his face. "I'll talk to him later. Let's work on your hand-to-hand combat skills. Those are definitely your most lacking right now."

Getting to my feet, I glanced at Caleb one more time, but he was already fighting. Hopefully, he could vent some of his frustration in practice.

Nico and I faced off, hands up by our faces.

"No magic," he ordered me. "Not that you could use any right now anyway."

I shook my head. "Definitely drained."

"Good," he said, "that means you won't cheat." He threw a punch at my face and I ducked beneath, trying to hit him with an uppercut, but he twisted out of the way.

Nico was definitely holding back, but even these slowed down fights were helping me learn how to react, block, and counter. The person I was a year ago would have gotten her ass kicked by the me now.

Caleb yelled out and I turned to see what happened.

Nico's fist connected with my face and I fell to the ground. "Shit, Ember, I'm sorry."

Head spinning, I tried to orient myself. Cold grass

pressed against my face and legs, which meant I was laying on the grass.

"What the fuck?" Caleb snarled. He pressed a hand to my face. "Shit, Dad. Did you have to hit her so hard?"

"She got distracted and didn't block," Nico said.

Finally, no longer spinning, I sat up and hissed at the throbbing in my face. "He didn't do anything wrong. The whole point of these is to teach me not to do stupid things like drop my hands and look away from my opponent."

Caleb probed at my face and I hissed in pain. "Let's get you some ice."

"Why did you yell out?" I asked.

"Got cut by a claw," he said. "It's healing."

"Why don't I heal fast like you guys do if I'm also a shifter?" I asked as I walked on wobbly legs into the house, Caleb's arm around my waist.

"We aren't really sure, honestly. There's no reason you shouldn't heal fast. Nana Kara was going to look into it for us."

Entering the kitchen, Jolie and Branson looked up from cleaning the dishes, the two having drawn the short straws after breakfast.

Jolie gasped. "Ember! What happened?"

Branson rushed to the freezer to get an icepack.

"I got distracted and Nico's fist didn't," I joked and laughed, but then hissed in pain at the movement.

"Where's Fox?" she asked Caleb.

"He went to take care of something in the city," Caleb answered.

"It's okay," I said. "The ice will help."

"Been punched in the face before?" Caleb asked with a frown.

I nodded. "Branson woke up swinging."

Branson held out the icepack with a flinch. "Yeah, sorry about that."

"To be fair, I learned to restrain people after that. Waking up in a strange house with IVs hooked up to you is bound to startle a lot of people."

"Oh, that would be terrifying," Jolie said with a nod.

Taking the icepack, I pressed it to my face and sighed.

"No more practice for you," Caleb ordered me.

"I just need a short break and then I can –"

"We don't know if you have a concussion or not. You hit the ground hard, too. We'll take you to Nana if Dad doesn't come back soon."

"You're worrying too much," I said and shook my head.

"I'd rather be too cautious than not enough," he said, stroked a hand down my hair, and walked out.

"He's acting weird today," Branson commented.

"I think he had a nightmare or something," I told them.

"Twitching in his sleep?" Jolie asked.

"Woke up growling."

She chuckled. "Yeah, that's usually a sign they had a bad dream." Her eyes widened and she turned in the direction he'd gone. "Oh. Um, I'll be right back."

She hurried away, wiping her hands on a dish towel as she left.

"Now she's acting weird," Branson said and laughed softly. "You sure you are okay?"

I nodded. "I'll sit on the stool here so if I faint or something you are nearby, okay?"

He nodded. "Thanks." Resuming doing the dishes, I watched him work and smiled. The shy, quiet bear had changed a lot recently. In doing jobs for Dan and spending time with alphas there, he was coming out of his shell bit by bit. I liked that he participated with us more, joking, and teasing.

"Are you excited for the house?" I asked. Rhys was an architect and with Caleb's directions had drafted the plans for our house. They wouldn't let me see them, but Dan had confirmed that construction had started on it not long after that and the house should be ready to move into in a month.

It was insane to think a year had already passed since I'd met Caleb and been dragged into all of this. Also frustrating that it was taking us so long to defeat the H.E.

"Yeah, I liked the apartments, but didn't really like being in the city. It's so noisy," he said as he scrubbed a plate.

"It's going to be great to be back in the trees," I agreed. "Naps under the stars and in a hammock sound fantastic."

He spun around. "No sleeping. If you have a concussion that —"

"I'm not tired right now, Branson. I was just saying I'm looking forward to that."

He exhaled harshly and turned back around. "It'll be nice to have true pack territory. Woods that are ours."

"You think many other hybrids will join us?" It was something I'd been thinking about a lot since my birthday. No one really knew how many hybrids existed. It could be ten or ten thousand.

"I think a lot will join us," he said with a nod. "We don't really have a place elsewhere, and it's nice to have somewhere to belong."

My insecurities reared their heads. "You don't think there might end up being a female hybrid that's more suited for you out there, do you?"

He looked over his shoulder and smiled. "No, I don't think there might be."

Sighing, I put my elbow on the counter and said, "Sorry, insecurities acting up."

"You are free to ask me for reinforcement compliments whenever you want, babe."

"Reinforcement compliments?" I asked.

"Like, 'yes, you are the most beautiful woman I know.'"

I scoffed. "That's obviously a lie. We have Leona over often."

"She's beautiful, but not as beautiful as you," he said.

"Well, I appreciate the compliment even if I don't quite believe it."

His cell phone rang and he dried his hands off. "Hello? Yes, sir. Okay. Okay, see you soon."

"Another job for Dan?" I guessed.

He nodded. "Sorry."

I waved his apology away. "You obviously enjoy it and I like how much more often you smile now."

"You should go sit outside so you aren't alone just in case you do have a concussion," he urged.

"Okay," I agreed and headed out of the kitchen and outside.

Triston and Riddick were sparring together while Jolie,

her mates, and Caleb stood off to the side talking in a circle, all scowling.

I sat on one of the lawn chairs, still holding the ice pack to my face.

"You okay?" Riddick asked as he and Triston took a break to drink some water, sweat pouring down their chests.

"Mmhmm," I said as I enjoyed seeing them shirtless and sweaty. So many muscles. "Branson is going to help Dan with something so I came out here because they're worried I might have a concussion. I don't think I do, but I figured you would all feel better if I was in line of sight."

"Thanks," Triston said with a smile. "You figured right."

"What are they talking about?" I asked and tilted my chin towards the other group.

Triston and Riddick shrugged.

"Royal things?" Triston suggested, which made the three of us laugh.

"You sure that you are alright?" Riddick asked.

I nodded. "The ice is helping."

"Shout if you need anything," Triston said, and then pounced on Riddick.

Getting to watch them spar was great, to witness the banter, the teasing, the fun they had as they practice fighting. The two of them were definitely much closer than they had been two months ago, which I supposed was to be expected.

An SUV pulled into the drive and Ezio rolled down the window to wave.

"Keep him safe!" I ordered him.

He saluted me a Branson climbed into the passenger seat.

"Another task for Dan?" Jolie asked as she sat beside me.

"Yep," I replied and immediately scowled. "It seems like everyone has something except me. Isn't there more I can do to help out? Should I get a job?" Was it even possible for me to have a job when my adoptive parents wanted me dead?

"You help out plenty at the house and you've been helping me plan Dan's birthday, which is a huge undertaking, and I'd be going insane without your help," she countered.

"If only I was crafty like Kieran and could sell things that I made," I said.

"Money is not an issue, Ember. We could give you monthly pay for the next thirty years without dipping into our savings. They make a lot of money with their businesses."

I sighed. "I feel useless, Jolie. Don't you understand?"

She laughed and nodded. "I do understand where you are coming from. I think once you move out to your land and have your tasks to perform out there that you'll feel better. It should only be another month before the house is ready."

With the pack having property now, I could sell my land and use that money wisely. That was the perfect idea!

"Do you know a real estate agent?" I asked.

She smiled wide. "I'm married to one, why do you ask?"

"What? Who is the real estate agent?"

"Fox. He got his license because he was bored and occasionally helps people find houses that are moving out of the pack areas."

"Well, I was thinking about selling my property," I explained.

Her eyes widened and she leaned close to me to whisper, "Are you planning to agree to be mated to the four gentlemen who have been courting you?"

"I am planning to live on the pack lands," I said instead of answering her, but gave her a wink.

She squealed, jumped to her feet, and started dancing around in a circle.

"What's got Mom so excited?" Caleb asked.

Grabbing my hand, she dragged me inside of the house and upstairs to her room. "Okay, if you're going to do it, you need to do it in an epic way."

"They haven't talked amongst themselves yet," I reminded her. "Two of them haven't confirmed if they want to be mated to me."

She scoffed and rolled her eyes. "I can tell you with one thousand percent confidence that all four of them want to be mated to you. Now, how are you going to reveal it? When? Where?"

"Um, honestly, I was going to wait until we defeated the H.E."

"That could be years from now, Ember. You can't let enemies ruin your personal life."

She did have a point. "What about next month?" I suggested.

"Is next month an important date of some kind?" she asked.

"It's the one-year anniversary of meeting Caleb and when we are supposed to move into the pack house," I explained.

She gasped. "A year already? Wow, it felt like so much

less time. Okay, that's actually pretty perfect. I'll drop a hint that it's your one-year anniversary and find out where they plan to take you. Then, we can come up with the plan on how you can reveal it to them. Oh, man this is going to be so much fun! We should include Leona, too. What do you think?"

"I'd love any help you two are willing to provide me. I'm a bit out of my depth when it comes to this. I was just going to tell them that I've decided to accept them," I admitted with a shrug.

"Oh! Oh, I need to get you a crown made. Oh, man. It's got to be even more epic than the one Nico was designing for me."

"A crown?" I asked, eyes wide.

"You're going to be Queen of the Hybrids, remember?"

My throat dried up and I stared in wide-eyed horror. "Um, no," I squeaked, "I hadn't remembered that part of this."

She patted my hand. "It'll be okay. You'll adapt quickly."

"I can't be a queen," I said and stood, pacing in front of her bed. "I'm not queen material."

"You are going to be a perfect queen, Ember. All you have to do is support Caleb and look out for your people, something you already do."

"Queen?" I squeaked. This was absolutely insane. I was just a nobody. A random discarded girl her parents didn't want.

Jolie set her hands on my arms, stopping my pacing. "Deep breath. Listen to me, you're not going to be thrown into this blindly. You've got me and you've got the acceptance of all of the kings already. We all view you as our daughter already, so you'll be fine. Okay?"

"As your daughter?" I asked, shocked at the sentiment.

Her smile softened and she nodded. "Yes, silly girl. Why do you think I told you that even if you left Caleb you would always be welcomed here? I view you as my new daughter and I will do everything within my power to help you. Okay? So, don't fret about the queen stuff. That'll happen much later anyway."

"Right," I breathed and nodded. The icepack had melted now, so pulled it away from my face.

She flinched. "We definitely need to get that healed. It looks bad."

"It doesn't hurt anymore," I said, but didn't touch it.

"Let me call Fox, if he doesn't answer I'll call Kara," she said and pulled out her phone.

After she got off the call with them, I asked, "Why were you all huddled together earlier? Why did you run out of the kitchen when I told you about his dream?"

"I have a power that doesn't manifest often, but occasionally shows up and terrifies me. I am worried that his bad dream is actually him using that power."

"Why are you being vague?" I asked with a growl. "What power?"

"Premonition," she answered. "I have dreams that sometimes come true."

"What was his dream?" I asked with a frown.

"That you end up sacrificing yourself to save them," she answered.

Well, fuck.

TWENTY-THREE

"We're going on an adventure," Jolie informed us one weekday morning where we were all lounging on the couch watching television.

"What kind of adventure?" Caleb asked, eyes narrowed.

"One to allow Ember to experience more of the world and the fun things we take for granted. Get ready. Wear comfortable clothes and tennis shoes."

"I hate when she's vague," Caleb groaned and got up to go change since he was still in his sweats.

Triston pulled me onto his lap sideways and kissed my cheek. "Since I'm changed, I get to have kissy time."

Turning my face, I kissed his lips and said, "Kissy time is one of my favorite times."

"Same," he said and kissed me harder.

"Come on, you two help us carry things to the car," Rhys ordered.

"Cockblocker," Triston whispered making me laugh.

"What was that?" Rhys asked, growling softly.

"You're a very scary and powerful alpha," Triston said as he stood and set me on my feet.

"Mmhmm," Rhys muttered. "I think you're getting a little too cocky and we might need to spar tomorrow."

"Ember!" Jolie called from the kitchen. I went inside and took the box she handed me. "To the car," she ordered.

"Yes, ma'am!" I shouted and hurried out, smiling as I heard her laughter behind me.

The boxes were closed, so I had no idea what they were bringing or had any clues as to where we were going.

Once everyone was finally ready, and in the SUVs, we headed out to our surprise destination.

We had to take two due to how many of us there were, but instead of Ezio or Martin driving, Deryn drove us.

"What's it like being a prince and second to someone like Dan?" Branson asked Deryn.

"Taxing," Deryn said with a laugh. "Dad is great. He is a fantastic alpha and does everything he can to keep his people happy and safe. He has amazing ideas and like a dozen different businesses that make him money with little involvement from him. It ends up requiring me to manage it, but it's good experience so I am prepared to take over."

"Has he ever overreacted so strongly you thought he might go rogue?" Branson asked.

Deryn nodded. "He thought Jolie was dead one time and destroyed his house."

"What?" I gasped.

"Yeah, we've had to rebuild that house at least six times. Three of them because of Jolie. He loves her like his own."

"Do you ever disagree with his decisions?" Branson asked.

Why was Branson asking so many questions like this? Was it from spending time with Dan or was he trying to find a way to say something to Caleb? Did he not agree with Caleb about something? Was it … me? Did he not agree with taking me as a mate?

Riddick set his hand on my leg and turned to face me. "What's wrong?"

I shook my head, not able to say anything.

He stroked his hand down my face and said, "Whatever you are thinking about, stop. We are here, you are safe, we are safe, and we are going to go have a fun day. Okay?"

Right. I needed to think about the here and now. Not what might or might not happen.

"Sorry," I whispered.

He kissed the side of my head and stroked his thumb over my thigh. "Don't apologize for having feelings."

Two hours later, we finally stopped … at a skating rink.

"What is this?" I asked.

"Ta da!" Jolie shouted. "We rented the entire rink so that we could take you skating."

"Really, Mom?" Caleb grumbled. "This is something you do as child—"

"I've always wanted to go skating!" I shouted and clapped my hands together.

Jolie poked Caleb in the side. "See?"

"You've never been skating?" Triston asked.

I shook my head. "We didn't do outings at the academy I went to. There weren't birthday parties or events like this. I thought it was something only humans did."

"Boys, carry the boxes inside," Jolie ordered them, slung her arm through mine, and pulled me inside.

A balding man in a polo shirt bowed when we entered. "Greetings."

"Is everything ready?"

He nodded. "The DJ is ready and waiting."

"Great!" she chirped. "Let's go get our skates on."

After finding skates in our size, we put them on and tied them. When she helped me get to my feet, I yelped as one skate went one way and the other went the other way, trying to make me do the splits.

She laughed and righted me. "Move them slowly," she advised. "Like this."

After watching her a bit, I tried to mimic her and was a bit successful. The guys carried in the stuff and I watched as they set up a large buffet area where we could get food and drinks as we wanted.

The DJ started playing popular music and lights began moving around the oval rink in the center.

"When you first go out there, just hold onto one of their hands and let them move you around so you can get a feel for it," she advised me.

I nodded. "Okay."

Triston zoomed by us with his skates on, spinning in a circle with a smile on his face. "I love skating."

"Show off," I muttered.

Caleb got his skates and immediately went out onto the

rink, skating fast, spinning, and showing off just as much as Triston.

Branson came to me, grabbed my hand, and winked. "I'll help you. Come on."

Slowly, he got me out onto the rink, the surface much slicker than the carpet we had been on, and I had a death grip on his hands.

We made our way around the rink and Jolie's mates joined us. Fox showed off the most, doing jumps and shit.

After several more laps, I finally got a little courage and started skating while just holding one of Branson's hands as he skated next to me.

"There you go," he praised.

Smiling like a fool, I let them teach me something I should have enjoyed as a child, happy to learn something new.

"I need a drink," I said and headed towards the side, but quickly realized I didn't know how to stop. "Shit!" I yelled as I raced towards the wall.

"Got ya!" Riddick yelled as he grabbed me just before I slammed into the wall and spun us around until I slid to a safe stop.

"Thanks," I whispered, breath fast and heart pounding.

"Tilt one foot forward to slow down," he advised and I looked down to see the weird thing on the front.

"Okay."

"You good?" he asked.

Holding the wall with a death grip, I nodded as I made my way off the rink and towards the food area.

After a bottle of water and a few finger foods, I turned around to look at the rink where everyone was smiling and racing around.

Pulling out my phone, I snapped a picture and immediately saved it as my phone's background. Pure, unadulterated bliss was on their faces and it was one of the most beautiful things I had ever witnessed.

"So, what do you want to do next?" Deryn asked from beside me as he ate some food, too.

I thought about it a moment, picturing all the things I saw people do on movies or had heard about throughout my years. What was something else I wanted to do? "Snow skiing?" I asked. "There was snow at my place, but I avoided it due to it being cold, and I've always wanted to try skiing."

"We can do that," he said with a nod. "I think you'll particularly love sledding."

"That does look fun!" I exclaimed, recalling a move we watched where they'd done a lot of sledding down hills.

"I'm really glad you're here, Ember," Deryn said. "You've made a significant change on Caleb's life. Something we experienced with Jolie. I'm glad to see my son experiencing the same."

"I'm glad I'm here as well," I said with a nod.

"If there's ever anything you want or need, don't hesitate to ask, okay?"

I laughed softly. "He built a house in the way I requested. I know he'll do a lot for me."

"You let us know, too, okay? Being with alphas is wrought with issues and especially when one or more are royals. We're here for you whenever you need us."

"Thanks," I said and smiled at him. "I appreciate that."

And I truly did. It was nice to know I had so many people to support me now.

For the first time, I felt like I truly could take on the world.

TWENTY-FOUR

"Why are we going to the City Hall again?" Ezio asked.

"I am changing my name and getting new ID cards," I reminded him.

"You know you could just let one of the princes handle it, right?" he asked as we drove at a snail's pace through downtown traffic.

"Why would I bother them with something so trivial when I am more than capable of doing it myself? I was doing things like this long before I met you all."

"Just accept it, Ezio. We have," Riddick said.

Branson huffed from the front seat. "We don't like it, but we've accepted it."

"You all didn't have to come," I reminded them. "You decided to join me all on your own. I was fine going with just Ezio."

"With someone ordered to murder you, we aren't going

to let you go anywhere without proper protection," Riddick said sternly.

"I'd likely draw less attention and be less recognized if I didn't have all of you around me. At least with Caleb not here, we will draw less attention than normal." Caleb had wanted to come, but was busy with an urgent matter with Nico that he couldn't leave. He had tried to convince me to wait, but I had to get my new ID and driver's license and go meet Fox to sign papers for selling my property. No one else knew I had sold my land yet, though. I was trying to keep it a secret.

"There are guards at City Hall all the time," Ezio reminded them. "It'll be safer there than the skating rink you went to last week."

"Pretty sure having Jolie and her mates with us was the most protected we could have been," I countered.

He sighed and shook his head, but didn't argue.

After finally finding a parking spot, Ezio got out first, checked the area, then opened our doors.

Carrying my folder with my birth certificate, original name change documents, and the new name change documents, I headed into the large building before us. City Hall was one of the oldest buildings in Jinla, and while I understood them keeping it due to it being historic, the boring box-shaped building wasn't exactly awe inspiring like some of the others. Like the library with castle tower corners.

Most of the people walking around wore suits, going about their political jobs, but there were a few dozen like me in regular clothes trying to get personal items accomplished.

I got into line and bounced on my toes as we waited.

Several people looked our way and I knew they weren't looking at me, but the handsome men behind me.

That's right, look all you want, but they're mine. I smiled wide and rocked on my feet, a happy tune whose lyrics I couldn't remember repeating in my head.

"Next!" an older man with glasses and a staff leaned against the counter beside him called.

Hurrying up to the counter, I pulled out my documents and turned them to face him. "Good morning, I'm here to change my name and get new IDs," I informed him.

He silently inspected my documents, his eyes widened, and he glanced up at me. After a moment of staring, he asked, "Do you have your old IDs to turn in?"

I took them out of my pocket and set them on the counter next to the documents. Why was he looking at me so strangely? Was it because of the name change signed by Silverowl? I doubted they saw very many of those.

"Give me just a few minutes to enter this into the system," he said and started typing on the computer.

Branson stood behind me, his back to mine as he kept watch and protected my blind spot.

"How are you paying the fee?" the man asked.

"Cash," I said and pulled it out of my pocket, counting it out before setting it in his hand.

"Perfect," he said with a nod and resumed typing.

A smattering of gasps and excited chatter started the instant I felt him through our connection.

Sighing softly, I shook my head. Of course he came.

Branson shifted to the side as Caleb stepped up behind me and he set his hands on my hips.

"Hello," I greeted without turning around.

"You felt me?" he guessed.

I nodded.

"Y-Your Highness," the man greeted nervously and bowed his head.

"Hello," Caleb greeted him. "Thank you for your hard work and for taking care of her."

"I-I'm just doing my job, sir."

Turning around, I looked up at him, and my eyes widened at the blood smeared on his face. "What happened?" I asked and reached towards it.

He shrugged. "Just a scratch."

"H-Here," the man said and set a pack of wet wipes on the counter next to me.

"Thank you," I said, took one, and wiped the blood of his face.

Caleb smiled wide as I did it, his hands squeezing my hips.

"Did you make your dad teleport you here after you finished your task?"

Caleb shrugged a shoulder. "Maybe."

Sighing, I shook my head. "I have four people guarding me and you still didn't trust me to be safe?"

"I'll always be worried when you aren't with me," he said. "Plus, I just wanted to see you. You've been helping Mom finalize Papa Dan's birthday and haven't had much time for me."

Pushing his chin, I made him tilt it up so I could wipe the blood splatters on his neck. "Sorry. Do you want to hangout tonight? We could watch a movie or play games."

"Yes." He grabbed my hand and lowered it. "How about dinner and a movie?"

"Okay, you're all entered in the system," the man said. "You just need to go down to room two hundred to take your picture for your IDs. They'll print them in the same room."

I spun around, closed the wet wipe package he'd offered us, and slid it to him, then gathered all of my documents and put them in the folder. "Thank you for your help. Have a great day."

He bobbed his head quickly. "You're welcome."

Caleb walked ahead of me, gathering lots of attention, but thankfully since he was ahead of me, they didn't stare at me.

It took us ten minutes to get the picture taken and my IDs printed. Part of the reason it took that long was because the employees were so nervous having Caleb there. I didn't understand the nervousness since he just sat calmly in the room and didn't even watch them.

Finished, I checked the time and smiled. "Great, let's head to our next stop," I told Ezio.

He nodded and we all walked out to the SUV.

"What's your next stop?" Caleb asked.

"I'm meeting Fox," I answered.

His brows rose. "Why?"

"It's a secret," I sang.

"You're not supposed to keep secrets from your pack," Triston said.

We resumed crawling through downtown traffic, though it wasn't as bad now that it was within working hours.

"It's fine," I said.

"If Fox is helping her, I'm sure it's fine," Ezio said, trying to help me.

"I think my fathers and I need a talk," Caleb grumbled.

Sighing, I shook my head. "Remember how you were irritated that your parents treat you like you're five sometimes? Have you forgotten that I'm thirty and have been handling my own shit most of my life?"

"You are part of a pack now, which means you don't have to handle your own shit now," Caleb countered.

My head fell back and I closed my eyes. "I swear, you males are so insufferable."

"You pronounced invaluable wrong," Triston said.

Ezio laughed.

"Come on, what are you up to?" Caleb asked.

"None ya," I replied with a wide smile.

We pulled into the parking garage and made our way up in the elevator to the office Fox had told me to meet him at, which turned out to be Rhys's architect firm.

Rhys and Fox looked up from a blueprint they were reviewing on the table and smiled at us.

"Morning," I greeted as we walked in.

"What's he doing here?" Fox asked as he looked at Caleb.

Caleb folded his arms across his chest. "You're meeting with the woman I'm courting behind my back. I came to ensure you aren't putting her in danger."

Fox scowled. "Rude."

Rhys shook his head and sighed. "I can't believe you're so untrusting of your own fathers."

"I'm untrusting of anyone when it comes to her," Caleb said.

Walking forward, I showed Fox my new ID. "Name change and new IDs are complete."

"Perfect!" he said, took the ID from me, and headed towards a copying machine. "I'll scan this and you can sign the papers."

"Sign what papers?" Caleb asked.

"You want to tell them?" Fox asked.

"No," I replied. "I don't want to tell them."

"What are you up to, Ember?" Branson asked. "Are you planning an escape or something?"

"You think his dads would help her plan that?" Triston asked.

"Of course we would," Rhys and Fox said simultaneously.

"See," Branson said.

"If she wants to leave you, that is up to her," Rhys said.

Caleb growled.

"I'm not planning an escape," I shouted. "Geez, you guys are ridiculous."

"Quite the opposite," Fox mumbled. "Sign here," he ordered me.

I signed the documents and confirmed my new banking information. I had needed to get a new account that wasn't connected to my adoptive parents on the off chance they remembered they had access to it and drained my accounts.

"Congratulations, Rubyhare!" Fox said loudly and hugged me.

"Thank you for your help, Fox."

"Are you going to tell us now?" Riddick asked.

I spun around and said, "Nope."

All four growled.

Laughing at their faces, I shook my head. "You four are such typical alpha males. I swear. Can't you just accept that I'm doing something that will be a good surprise and leave it alone?"

"A good surprise?" Triston asked.

"Yes," I said with a nod.

"That you'll eventually reveal to us?" Caleb asked.

I nodded again. "It's part of a surprise I've been planning for several weeks. You don't want to spoil my surprise, do you?"

"Sort of," he mumbled.

"The wait will be worth it," Rhys said and clapped him on the shoulder. "I promise."

"Does everyone know but us?" Riddick asked.

Rhys, Fox, Ezio, and I nodded.

"Wow, that's so rude," Branson said.

"No, it's great because she's asking for help to do something that she wants to be special. You should be excited, not irritated," Ezio told them. "If I had a woman involving all of my family to help her do something for me, I would be ecstatic. Ember, if you end up changing your mind, call me." Caleb growled and Ezio raised his hands and backed up a step. "I'm just teasing. Chill."

"No offense, but you are a little too old for me," I said with a smile at Ezio.

"Do you have anything else you need to do?" Triston asked.

"Yes, I need to go to the house," I answered. "I'm starving."

"Come here really quick," Rhys called to me. "I wanted to show you the draft I have."

"Of the healer's cabin?" I asked, excited.

He nodded. "Kara and I worked on it for several hours."

"I'm so excited!" I gasped and looked over the blueprint he had started. It was definitely a better setup than my barn and house had been. "This is going to be perfect."

"I'm glad you like it," Rhys said.

"Come on, we've got to get you home before your stomach comes to live and eats us," Triston teased as my stomach growled loudly again.

"Bye," I waved to Fox and Rhys who had started back on the blueprint they'd been reviewing when we'd walked in.

They waved and I skipped out of the office and to the elevator.

"What do you want to eat when we get to the house?" Riddick asked.

"Hm, sandwiches of some kind," I suggested.

"Okay," he said with a nod.

"Club sandwiches," Branson suggested.

"Oh, yes, that," I agreed and nodded.

We started our drive home, but the traffic came to a full stop and didn't move at all. People ahead of us started getting out of their vehicles.

"What's going on?" I asked.

"I'm going to find out," Caleb said and got out of the SUV. He shifted into his wolf form and trotted through the stopped cars.

We all watched, waiting for something.

A giant black hound the size of a house jumped into the

roadway and howled. The sound sent the hair on my nape on end and my instinct was to flee.

"What is that fucking thing?" Branson asked.

"Demon hound," Ezio growled. "We've got to kill it before it hurts others. Branson, Riddick, with me."

"I'm not staying in the fucking car," I told him and climbed out. "We don't split the group anymore."

"Come on, stay at my side, okay," Triston said, grabbed my hand, and we ran to assist Caleb, who was fighting the hound in his warrior form.

Ezio shifted, climbed atop a nearby SUV, and used it to jump up onto the hound's back.

"We're going to make sure the civilians are far enough away for safety," I told Branson and steered Triston towards a mother and daughter hunkered down by a wall trying to hide from the demon hound and stay out of sight.

Rhys flew down from the sky over our heads and Fox leapt off of his back, a sword in his hand, joining the fight against the demon hound.

"Come with us," I ordered the mother.

She picked up her daughter, and ran away from the hound, towards safety, with Triston and I behind her until she was far enough that we knew we could head back.

Thankfully, there weren't any others nearby in danger, so we waited nearby, watching as they worked together to carve into the hound.

The thing was bleeding like crazy, but its blood was black and looked inky.

"Where did that come from?" I asked Triston.

"I don't know much about demons because they're rare. I

just know they're strong and cause a lot of trouble when they do show up."

"Status?" Jolie asked behind us.

I yelped and spun around to see her and Nico behind us.

"Just the one demon hound that we've seen. We evacuated the civilians that were nearby," Triston answered.

She nodded. "I'll stay here with them."

Nico nodded and strode forward with a staff in his hand, sending fireballs and other spells at the demon hound in areas the others weren't attacking it. Its large size was definitely a disadvantage to it.

"Has it spoken?" Jolie asked.

"Demons speak?" I asked, shocked.

She shrugged. "It's an animal so I thought maybe you heard it."

I shook my head. "Not so far it hasn't."

"Maybe demons are different," Triston suggested.

"Does this happen often?" I asked her.

"Demon hounds? No, we don't encounter demons very often."

"No, fighting random battles in the city," I amended.

She nodded. "At least once every three months."

That explained how quickly they all moved into action and converged to fight it.

"Is it something about this city?" I wondered.

"We think it's partly because of how many people live here of different races, but it is also the most populated city within one hundred miles. It draws the attention of those who want to cause trouble."

The hound fell to its knees and howled.

Rhys vaulted Fox up in the air, high over the hound's head. Fox did a flip and brought his sword down, decapitating it.

The body wavered and then disappeared in a puff of black smoke.

"Well, that was quick," I said.

Jolie clapped and cheered. "Good job, guys!"

Fox bowed with a hand flourish and Caleb rolled his eyes at his father.

"I say we get ice cream!" Fox shouted as he jogged over to Jolie, kissing her cheek.

"We haven't eaten lunch yet," she reminded him.

"We were going to make club sandwiches when we got back to your place," Triston informed her.

She smiled. "Sounds great to me!"

"Then ice cream?" Fox asked.

"Sure," she agreed.

"Sundaes?" I suggested.

Fox nodded. "I knew I liked you."

Caleb walked over, bent and whispered in my ear, "Only if we take a spare can of whipped cream back to your room after."

My face heated and I said, "And chocolate syrup."

He nipped my earlobe gently and said, "Agreed."

"What are we celebrating?" Nico asked.

"Rubyhare's official name change and whatever secret thing she did with dad," Caleb answered as he climbed into the SUV.

"Is it just killing you not to know?" Jolie teased. "You

poor man, having to wait to know something. Sorry I spoiled him so much, Ember. It's my fault he can't handle surprises."

"It's okay," I said with a shrug. "It'll make the reveal that much better."

"When is this reveal?" Triston asked as he pushed me into the SUV.

"Soon," I replied vaguely.

"See you at the house," Nico said and teleported Rhys, Fox, and Jolie away.

"He could have teleported us," Caleb said with a loud sigh.

"And leave me all alone?" Ezio said with a pout. "So rude, nephew."

"Let's go," Caleb replied. "Fighting that thing worked up my appetite." He looked down at me and winked.

Yeah, my appetite had increased, too, but for dessert.

CHAPTER
TWENTY-FIVE

The holidays were fast approaching, so on top of worrying about our anniversary, I was worrying about what to get each of them.

I holed up in my room, scouring the internet for ideas, watching holiday movies, and had a notebook slowly filling up with them.

The problem was that they didn't really have anything they *wanted*.

What did you get someone who had everything?

My crafting skills were incredibly limited.

"It's hopeless," I groaned and dropped my head to *thunk* against my desktop.

Someone knocked on the door. Quickly, I hid the notebook and put it in the drawer of the desk before turning and calling out, "It's open."

"What happened to your head?" Riddick asked as he walked in.

"Oh, nothing, what's up?"

"The four of us are going to be gone for a bit. We just wanted to make sure you were okay to stay here or if you wanted one of us to stay." He sat on the edge of my bed and smoothed down the comforter.

"Where are you guys going?" I asked and sat next to him.

"It's a secret," he said and tugged at a frayed corner of the comforter.

My eyes narrowed in suspicion. "A secret, huh? One you suddenly have after I wouldn't tell you what I did with Fox?"

Laughing softly, he pinched the tip of my nose. "We're going shopping for holiday presents."

"Oh," I said and rubbed my nose. "I see."

He frowned and canted his head slightly. "Something's upsetting you?"

"I was trying to figure out holiday shopping myself," I admitted and dropped my head to look at my hands in my lap. "I've never bought gifts for others, so I'm not really sure what to get. I've been researching on the internet and movies and ... and ..."

He set his hand on top of mine. "You don't have to get us anything at all, but we will be happy with whatever you get us, Ember."

"I'll figure it out," I said and gave him my best smile. "I've just got to consider what each of you likes."

"We like you," he said and kissed me. "You're definitely my favorite thing I've found this year." Laying me down, he draped himself half over my body, slid his hand along my face, and kissed me again. He licked at the seam of my lips and I opened for him, our tongues moving together in a slow, sensual dance as my hands curled in his shirt.

"Ezio is waiting for us," Triston said. "Oh, I see the delay. Please continue."

Riddick sat back and kissed my cheeks. "I'm coming."

"Already? That's a bit fast even for you," Triston teased.

Riddick helped me sit up and kissed me quickly again before standing and adjusting himself. "Ha. Ha. Come on, let's go."

"Have fun!" I called after them.

Triston winked. "Behave while we're gone."

"No promises!" I yelled back.

Laying back on the bed, I exhaled harshly. While they were gone was the perfect time for me to do some online shopping. I just needed to figure out what to buy. Getting to my feet, I grabbed my notebook and phone, and headed downstairs to sit in the living room while I shopped.

Stopping in the kitchen, I grabbed snacks, and a drank, then plopped down on the couch. Maybe if I just focused on one of them at a time, I could narrow down the options and find something to buy.

Since I felt like Caleb would be the most difficult, he would be the last one. Triston was the first and I thought about all the things he liked and had started doing.

Ever since the trip to the Den's market, he had talked a lot of crafting. After a bit of searching, I found a wood carving kit.

Moving on to Branson, I found a leather braiding kit where I just needed to braid the leather strips together and add a metal charm to it. Fairly confident in my abilities to do something that simple, I added that to my cart next.

Riddick was a bit harder, since like Caleb he pretty much had everything he wanted.

"Ugh," I groaned and dropped my head back.

Deryn looked over me to the phone in my hand.

I screamed and fell off the couch as I jumped away from him.

"Sorry," he said with a chuckle.

Getting back onto the couch, I sighed. "I swear you all love scaring me."

He sat on the end of the couch and shrugged. "It is pretty comical. Are you trying to figure out holiday gifts?"

I nodded. "It's not as easy as the movies make it to be."

"Well, not when you have spoiled men like Caleb and Riddick it's not. Have you thought about just getting the leather bracelet kit to make them all the same thing? Having something handmade by you that is matching would make them all happy."

I hadn't thought about it because I was worried my skills wouldn't be enough, but braiding the leather strips didn't seem that hard. All the other crafty things I'd been looking at were like wood carving or other complicated ones. Could I do the bracelets?

"Even if they're rough, they'll love that you spent the time and energy to make it," he assured me.

"Won't they prefer getting different gifts? Isn't it a bit lame to get them all the same exact thing? Like a cope out?"

"It's a little different in a situation like this. If you got every single person you know the same thing, that might be seen as a cop out, but if you get your pack the same thing, they'll view it as a way to increase your bond."

That did make sense.

"What if I can't do it?"

He shrugged. "Then keep a backup list of things to order. Buy one and give it a try and then decide. You can get that first kit with one-day shipping, try out the kit, and then if you do well, order more. Or if you can't do it, or feel like it's not good enough to your standards, hop back on to order other items."

"Okay," I agreed with a nod and rubbed at my chest, which was aching slightly.

"How are you doing while they're gone?" he asked.

"Uh, fine," I said and realized he was glancing at the way I was rubbing my chest. "It aches," I admitted.

"That makes sense. Caleb said the same when he was helping Nico the day you went to the City Hall."

"Does it get better or worse when you're mated?" I asked curiously. I had never had the chance to talk to a mated person and hadn't asked Leona or Jolie yet.

"Both." He laughed at my frown. "The first week after you are mated is one that requires you all to stay together or the pain is worse. After that, it starts to ebb and it is easier to be apart. I think because the bond settles fully and then you're able to feel each other better, so you don't have to be as worried about your mate being in danger without you knowing."

"I feel like a failure of an adult for not knowing so many things and being so sheltered," I admitted and sighed. "I could have gone out and experienced anything I wanted after I graduated, but ended up doing this to myself."

"Emotional trauma is a bitch," he said and shrugged.

"We all deal with it in our own way and you dealt with it by hiding. I have to say, you've come a long way in the past year, Ember. The amount of personal growth we've seen in you is amazing. We know we may treat you like children, but it's clear how mature you are. Especially, when it comes to protecting those you care about. Speaking of that, how are your healing practices doing?"

"I have a *long* way to go, but I was able to heal a dozen cuts on Fox simultaneously and a single, deep cut on Rhys."

"That's great," Deryn praised. "Caleb is constantly getting hurt just enough that his advanced healing takes longer to treat the types of wounds he gets, so having you there to speed up the healing will make me feel better."

"Can I ask you something personal?"

He nodded. "Shoot."

"Did you guys ever doubt that Jolie was the one?"

"No," he said with a shake of his head. "We always knew she was the one for us. There was a time we were hesitant to admit it, to ourselves and each other, but deep down all of us knew." His brows furrowed. "Did one of them say something to you?"

I shook my head. "Branson was asking Ezio about disagreeing with Dan as alpha over things so it made me wonder."

"That's your emotional trauma talking, but I see how you went there. Branson likely asked that because Dad was testing him the other day to see how Branson would respond in a situation where he didn't agree with what he was being ordered to do."

"Why would he do that?" I asked, confused.

"Dad has been trying to teach Branson what it's like to be an alpha beneath a king. There are times when your king gives you an order you don't agree with and you have to decide how to handle it."

"Still doesn't mean it wasn't about me," I pointed out.

"True, I don't know with one hundred percent certainty what any of them feels, but Branson looks at you like you are the light in the darkness, the same way my brothers look at Jolie."

Hearing him say that did make me feel better.

"Thanks, Deryn."

He patted my knee and stood. "Anytime, Ember."

Back to my phone, I ordered four of the leather bracelet kit. I would make them and do my best. That was all I could hope for after all.

That, and that the four of them would end up loving the gift as much as Deryn assured me they would.

CHAPTER
TWENTY-SIX

Branson lay on the floor of my apartment in bear form, while I was draped across him, enjoying the soft, furry bed he made.

"Are you going to go shopping with me this afternoon?" I asked him. The birthday for King Dan of the Werewolves, required me to wear a fancy dress, so I was being forced to go shopping yet again, since I didn't want to use the dress Leona had given me for my birthday as that was saved for our one-year anniversary when I was going to ask them to be my mates. I felt like I had done more shopping in the last two months than I had done in the previous ten years of my life. It really wasn't fair that the guys could wear the same suit to every event, but I had to get a new dress each time. Thankfully, I wasn't the one paying for it, but still.

Branson huffed. *"Yes, we are all going. Remember, no more splitting up the party?"*

Right, I had asked Caleb to keep us all together and he was doing his best to follow up on that promise.

"Sorry." I cringed. "I know dress shopping isn't your ideal day." Jolie and most of Caleb's family were working on the event, so we were on our own today.

"Watching you try on pretty dresses is definitely a good day for me."

Believing him was hard, but I wasn't going to argue.

"Only another week until we move into the new pack house," I reminded him with a wide smile. "I can't wait."

"It's going to be awesome. I still need to pack a bunch of things. I don't know how I ended up with so much stuff."

I laughed and nodded. "Same! I have a ton of things to pack to move over there."

Thankfully, we had several people to help us move things over. We had spent the past several weeks deciding on furniture and ordering it to be delivered to the house.

The guys had gone to inspect the house, but hadn't let me go with them, wanting the house to be a surprise for me once it was fully built.

To say I was anxiously awaiting the new house was an understatement. I was also anxiously awaiting our anniversary. Leona was hiding the mating stones for me to ensure the guys didn't find it before the day.

She had squealed more than Jolie and both of them went into uber planning mode to help me pull off a fun and exciting reveal.

I just hoped the guys would actually agree to be my mates. There was a slim chance that Branson and Triston would say no. Being my packmate, dating me, were far different than agreeing to be my permanent mate.

"Your heart is beating fast. What are you thinking about?" Branson asked.

"Sorry, just lots of things," I said to avoid answering. "Do you think I should wear something more conservative since it's Dan's birthday?" Normally, my dresses were a bit sexy, but this was a king's birthday and not a function like the others we had been to.

"I think you should wear whatever you want," he said. *"Whatever you are comfortable with. Pretty sure Dan wouldn't care if you showed up in sweats and a t-shirt."*

Laughing, I nodded. "You're right. I could see him just hugging me and disregarding whatever I wore."

My phone beeped and I fumbled towards the couch to get it, ultimately slipping off Branson and landing on the ground with an, "oomph." Finally grabbing my phone, I answered it.

"There's a hybrid under attack," Caleb said, his voice worried. "We're going to the park to try to help. Meet in the foyer."

"Understood," I said and hung up. "Come on, Branny Boy, we're going to help a hybrid."

Branson shifted into his human form, grabbed my hand, and tugged me out of his apartment.

Everyone was gathered in the foyer, and after making sure we were ready, Caleb led the way out of the apartment building. Moving at a quick pace, we maneuvered around people milling about, going about their evening, we tried our best to stay together. This part of the city was always bustling with activity in the evenings.

Branson kept hold of my hand, so we didn't get separated, and we grouped back up at the park with the others. Letting Caleb lead, since he said he could sense them, we went deeper into the large city park.

In the center of the park, on a grassy area surrounded by trees, we found a petite brunette woman with wide, terrified eyes, curled up, trying her best to keep the four people around her from kicking her in the head and stomach.

As soon as they saw what was happening, the four men around me shifted into warrior forms and ran forward to stop the attack.

I blinked, shocked they had left me alone to go after her. Shaking my head, I cleared the stupid thoughts, shifted myself, and leapt forward to grab her while my pack distracted the assholes attacking her. Picking her up, I leapt up into the air, over two of the attackers' heads, and carried her to a nearby tree since it was a distance away and a safer place. "Stay here, okay? They're going to deal with those assholes."

She panted, her body shaking and occasionally shifting into a weasel form. After a second, she turned into a full weasel. *"There's more! They're coming! They called for reinforcements!"*

Jerking my head up, I scanned the surrounding area and gasped as I saw the dozens of people approaching. "It's a trap!" I screamed.

Caleb's eyes darted towards me for a second before he looked around the area, finding the enemies approaching. "Move closer!" he ordered me.

"Come on," I ordered the woman and scooped her up into my arms. "We need to get closer to my pack."

"Pack?" she asked. *"There's a hybrid pack?"*

I nodded. "We'll talk after we get out of this."

Riddick grabbed me and jerked me forward, a clawed hand slashing down just behind me, nearly cutting through my shoulder. He snarled, punched the attempted attacker, and pushed me so I was in the center between Triston, Branson, and him.

People flooded into the park, too many for me to count.

The guys kept fighting, taking down opponents, but more replaced the ones they defeated.

"There's a ton of enemies," I gasped. "They are surrounding us." Was this the trap they'd been talking about the night I had spied on them? Was this the night they were going to try to kill us all?

"We know," Riddick growled.

"What are we going to do?" I asked. "There are too many."

Someone grabbed Riddick, yanked him away from us, and dragged him into the mob, separating us.

"Riddick!" I screamed.

Caleb roared and released a torrent of fire that burned four people in front of him, but several mages used shields to stop the fire from hurting others.

A strong hand gripped my hair and jerked me backwards, making me scream out and drop the weasel shifter woman. She was thankfully okay, but an electric shock through me made it hard to react in any way against my attacker.

Fists punched my side and try as I might, I couldn't get their hands off of me. There were just too many. I tried kicking with my powerful legs, but only managed to take out one or two people. Leaping up into the air, I was immediately pulled back down and claws slashed across my chest, opening large, gaping wounds. I screamed and stumbled to a knee, using roots from the ground to grab the person and force them to their knees. "Bastards," I growled.

"Ember!" Branson bellowed and tried to use his bear claws to tear through the people, but with mages, dragons, werewolves, and elves between us, it was near impossible.

Using my telekinesis, I started throwing people away from me, created dirt walls and shoved others away from me, and started pelting people with stones.

There were just too many, and I couldn't protect all sides of myself. For every person I'd send away from me, another would hit me from behind with a spell or their claws.

Within a matter of minutes, our pack was completely separated from each other.

Outnumbered, we were severely outnumbered. With so many people attacking, it made it hard to do anything except defend yourself.

After shifting into my small rabbit form, I darted through the legs of those around me, trying to get to my pack, to help them fight off their attackers and reunite us, so we could protect each other's backs and fight our way out.

Someone grabbed me by the scruff of my neck and I immediately shifted into warrior form, kicking them in the stomach and sending them flying away from me.

Three people surrounded me, walking in a slow circle with claws extended as they debated their best plan of attack. The brief reprieve gave me enough time to look for my men.

Branson was on the ground, two werewolves cutting into him with their claws. Riddick was surrounded by several mages, their spells forcing him to his hands and knees. Triston tried to shift and fly into the air, but was grabbed by another dragon and slammed into the ground. Caleb had five men on him, holding him down as the large bearded man with the scar raised a large, glowing sword over his head, preparing to decapitate him.

No. No! I would not watch the men I loved get slaughtered.

This was it. This was the time.

If I didn't act now, they were going to die. I couldn't let that happen. There was no telling if anyone was coming to our aid. It could be hours until backup showed up, if they did at all. This was up to us. We had to get away. I had to get them all to safety.

"Time for you to die," the mage my adoptive dad had ordered to kill me said, walking forward with a sword in his hand.

Drawing in a deep breath, I gathered all of my remaining magic, and looked at each of my men. Each was bleeding, eyes wide in panic, trying to protect themselves. I opened a portal beneath each of them. The weasel shifter screamed as she got kicked again, and I knew Caleb would be furious, but instead of creating a portal for myself, I opened a portal beneath the weasel shifter instead. All five portals were ready to open at Leona's house, in their backyard.

"No," I told the mage, gasping for breath as I struggled to hold all of the people back from the portals. "You may kill me, but you're not going to kill them."

"What are those?" someone asked, distracting the mage with the sword in front of me and pointing at my portals.

"Ember!" Caleb screamed, seeing the portal beneath him. The bearded man with the sword stumbled back, unsure what the portal was.

"I love you," I called back, tears streaming down my face.

"No!" Caleb, Riddick, Branson, and Triston yelled simultaneously.

"I love you all," I whispered, plunged them into the portals, and sealed them before any of the enemy could follow after. The minute they sealed, my magic drained out of me, and I barely had enough time to shift into my rabbit form to escape the people grasping me.

Hopping through their legs, my vision darkening and heart hammering so fast it felt like a hummingbird's, I maneuvered myself away from the ones who had seen me turn into a rabbit. I jumped up the legs of one man before hopping onto the shoulders of a woman, and jumping from head to head of the enemies there, trying to make my way through their forces. Hands grabbed at me, but I continued to push through, to escape.

The darkness encroached on my vision, and as I leapt, dizziness caused me to fall. My body shifted to my human form and someone grabbed me by the hair, jerking my head back and making me cry out. The mage spun his sword, about to stab me through the chest with it.

Purely running on adrenaline, I shifted into my rabbit form again and hopped through his legs. A group of people trapped me in a circle.

"It's over," the mage said.

The familiar call of a hawk sounded above me. Looking up, my rabbit brain screamed in fear as talons wrapped around me. The beat of wings took me up into the air. *"I've got you, Em,"* Kieran said telepathically. *"I'll take you to safety."*

Darkness surrounded me, cuddling me in its calming clutches.

Continue Ember's story in Outshone: https://catbanks.co/Ember

Join my newsletter: https://catbanks.co/Newsletter

Continue Ember's Story in Outshone (Her Royal Harem: Ember #3) catbanks.co/Ember

In the gripping finale of "Her Royal Harem: Ember," tensions escalate as Ember and her pack are thrust into the roles of King and Queen of the Hybrids, their reign teetering on the brink of destruction. The haunting specter of loss looms large, casting a shadow over their newfound sovereignty.

As Ember and her mates grapple with the aftermath of a brutal battle, the fragile peace is shattered by the arrival of an orphaned hybrid child. Can Ember and her mates navigate the uncharted waters of family life while holding their pack together?

To solidify their reign, Ember and her pack must attend the Summit. Here, the final remnants of the Hybrid Eradication (H.E.) launch a desperate assault, threatening not only Ember's pack, but the very fabric of unity among the Other clans.

Battles rage on multiple fronts - the war-torn landscape of their past, the uncharted mysteries of a distant island, and the uncharted territory of parenthood. The weight of destiny bears down on Ember's shoulders, and the question remains: will their pack crumble beneath the pressure, or will they rise to fulfill their destined place in history?

In this thrilling finale, "Outshone - Her Royal Harem: Ember" delivers a rollercoaster of emotions, action-packed sequences, and the powerful theme of resilience in the face of adversity. As Ember's pack confronts their inner demons and external foes, the choices they make will determine not just their own fates but the future of all hybrids. Will they succumb to the overwhelming challenges, or will they stand tall, united, and embrace the destiny that awaits them? Join Ember and her pack as they fight for their lives, their love, and the future of the hybrid clan.

Order Here: catbanks.co/Ember

CONNECT WITH CATHERINE BANKS

I really appreciate you reading my book! Here are some ways to connect with me:

www.catherinebanks.com

Join my newsletter for deals and snippets:

http://catbanks.co/newsletter

ABOUT THE AUTHOR

Catherine Banks is an award-winning, USA Today bestselling author who writes in several romance subgenres and has multiple pseudonyms. She began writing fiction at only four years old and finished her first full-length novel at the age of fifteen. She is married to her soulmate and best friend, Avery, who she has two amazing children with. After her full-time job, she reads books, plays video games, and watches anime shows and movies with her family to relax. Although she has lived in Northern California her entire life, she dreams of traveling around the world. Catherine is also C.E.O. of Turbo Kitten Industries™, a company with many hats including being a book publisher and store full of nerdy fun.